Desert Rose

by

J. Arlene Culiner

Blake's Folly Romance

Desert Rose

Cover Art by *Jennifer Greeff*

The Wild Rose Press, Inc.
PO Box 708
Adams Basin, NY 14410-0708
Visit us at www.thewildrosepress.com

Publishing History
First Edition, 2023
Trade Paperback ISBN 978-1-5092-4861-2
Digital ISBN 978-1-5092-4862-9

Blake's Folly Romance
Published in the United States of America

She'd been thinking about him, too? Imagining what his life was like in the same way he'd been thinking about her? Only there was a difference. He did the talking; she asked questions, kept the conversational ball rolling without giving out information.

He took in the flat planes of those wonderful cheekbones, the radiance in her eyes, and his heart warmed. How right it felt, sitting across the table from her. But he needed to know more. As gently as possible, he said, "Okay, it's your turn now."

Rose stared. "What's my turn?"

"You have a real knack for drawing people out. It's flattering, it won me over, and I'm not the only person you've captivated, either. But being a perfect listener can be a tactic."

"What's that supposed to mean?"

"It's a way to avoid talking about yourself."

"Ah." Rose looked down.

"I'm right, aren't I?"

"There's nothing interesting to say."

"Let me be the judge of that."

Silently, she folded her table napkin into a tiny square.

"Is there a dark secret you're hiding?"

Her eyes flicked up. Finally. "Fine. What is it you want to know?"

"Everything, of course." He smiled at her. "How about starting with essentials?"

She shrugged. "What sort of essentials?"

"You're hedging."

She looked away again, nodded. Looked back. Then grinned. "Guilty as charged."

Praise for J. Arlene Culiner

"A story of mature love, gender respect, with classic storytelling absent in so many books today. Kudos to J. Arlene Culiner!"

~ Lisa McCombs, Readers' Favorite

"Desert Rose is a delightful, charming read with bold characters that easily draw readers into their story. The author brings Blake's Folly and its inhabitants to life and manages to be both entertaining and emotional."

~ E.L. Hurley InD'tale Magazine

"I loved the depth of the characters, the quirky nature of the nearly abandoned town, and learning about fossils, rocks, and desert creatures. But mostly I enjoyed the slow-building romance."

~ Romance Fan

"Nothing is ever straightforward, otherwise, life would be too predictable. Deliciously hot and steamy love scenes complete the picture."

~ Jeanne Livingstone

Dedication

Many thanks to my editor, Eilidh MacKenzie,
to everyone at the Wild Rose Press,
and to Pascale Paumier's lovely baroque cello.

The white rabbit put on his spectacles. "Where shall I begin, please your Majesty?" he asked.

"Begin at the beginning," the King said, very gravely, "and go on till you come to the end: then stop."

Lewis Carroll,
Alice's Adventures in Wonderland

Chapter One: Second Hand Rose

When the bell above the shop door tinkled, Rose's well-practiced welcome smile was almost in place. Almost…then it stopped in mid-stretch. Stunned, she stared, swallowed, stared some more. My goodness: wasn't *he* gorgeous. Her interest increased, and her heart did a pitter-patter tippy-toe dance as she took him in: tallish—but anyone would be tall when compared to her tiny size—rangy, with tousled hair so black it appeared blue under the lights, an explorer's bone structure and weather-honed skin, deep brown eyes. And here she was, acting like a complete idiot, frozen into place, gawking at him as if he were of another species, or something totally new-fangled dropped down from a distant stretch of the Milky Way.

Not that he seemed to be faring any better, not moving, staring at her, his gaze unwavering, the wide-open door letting in frosty air and plump snowflakes. What was that gaze of his telling her? That he was surprised? Pleased? Oh yes. He liked what he saw, all right—and men did like her, she knew that. She was used to their admiration. They liked naturally golden curls, slanting blue eyes, and the broad, flat cheekbones of the Russian steppe. But wasn't it especially nice to be admired by such a gorgeous specimen? Yes, indeed.

Mentally, Rose shook herself, forced herself out of her stupor—somebody had to do something. This was a store, a business, not a blind date. If a man suddenly showed up in a ladies' dress shop, that meant there was already a woman in his life. Unless he was a cross-dresser. Or was lost and needed directions out of this half-a-horse hellhole.

"Hello." She forced the formerly incomplete smile into something more fulsome and professional.

"Hello," he answered. Smiled back. Not a forced smile, though. A wonderful one that softened the craggy angles of his face, crinkled into deep lines around his mouth and eyes.

Rose swallowed. Stared for another few seconds, then ordered herself to stop thinking about his smile, his lips, the bristly, salty way his skin would taste if she licked it, right there, at the corner of his mouth. The thought made her knees tremble. A bad case of lust at first sight? With a great effort of willpower, she corralled the lusty thoughts until they were more manageable, somewhat closer to normality. Heard her own voice, calm, practical: "Can I help you with something?"

He blinked, once, twice, as if waking from a trance. Then, laugh lines and crinkles disappeared, gave way to a more business-like expression. "Yes, of course." Stepping into what was left of the warmth in the shop, he turned, closed the door behind him. Stared at her again. Cleared his throat. "I'm looking for a present."

"For your wife?" Rose held her breath.

His mouth tightened. "Not quite."

"Ah." Hope faded. Not quite a wife wasn't nearly as bad as a snuggled-in official wife, but it was close enough. "Your fiancée." She was fishing, she knew, but hoped he didn't. Not that she was being subtle.

"No, not that either." His hand rose, then dropped: a confused gesture. "The woman I'm…ah…well…we live together. In the same apartment, that is."

"Ah." Okay. The woman he was living with. Hope skittered out of the picture with all the clang of a badly tuned wedding bell. Unless she'd detected—no, intuited—another note, one hinting that all wasn't entirely perfect.

She tucked that thought into the back of her mind, ready for perusal at some later moment. For now, he was a potential customer and nothing more, she scolded herself…aside from that first blinding moment when he'd opened the door and seen her. A moment that had been nothing less than a spontaneous gut-deep call of male to female, female to male. A call now quashed with the message of "too late, already taken."

"What sort of present were you looking for?" she managed to ask coolly enough.

"Damned if I know." The wonderful smile and the creases were back again. "I was hoping you could help me with that."

"Fine," she said, all efficiency. If a passionate romance were out of the question, a few bucks in her pocket would come in handy. Sales weren't an everyday occurrence in a dress shop way out in a semi-ghost town in the Nevada wasteland. She relied on the Internet for most of her profits. "Were you thinking of a dress? A blouse? What size does your…your, uh…lady friend take?"

"Actually, I didn't have clothing in mind." He looked around, unsure, taking in the bright fabrics, old-fashioned hats, the shoes of another era—all tucked in between heaped books, the occasional vase, and a

3

mountain of draped scarves, all displayed in a chaos of color. "Most of this is secondhand?"

"Vintage," Rose corrected. "The best."

He sighed, frowned. "Marina would never think of wearing previously owned clothes. Even beautiful vintage clothes. For her, everything has to be new and have a designer label."

"Oh, I see."

"I haven't offended you, I hope." He seemed sincere.

"Of course you haven't," Rose assured him. "We don't all have the same values, thank goodness." She could picture a woman named Marina: a snob. Pretentious and picky. What the hell was he doing with a woman like that? Look how he was dressed—in faded, tight blue jeans that hugged his slim hips and muscular legs, a well-worn black leather jacket, scuffed black boots. The thick woolen scarf wound around his neck still glinted with melted snow droplets. Sexy as hell.

"Amen," he seconded. "I don't have the same values as Marina either."

"Doesn't that bother you?" Rose stopped. Flushed. "I'm sorry. I have no right to ask that question. It was rude of me."

His unwavering eyes met hers. Then he chuckled softly.

"Okay." Rose scraped together some lost dignity. "Let's get back to the gift. What sort of woman is she? Does she like vintage jewelry? I have some nice pieces over here, in the display counter."

They were old pieces, in designs no longer made, but Rose had always prided herself on having a good eye and excellent bargaining skills. The result was, she'd managed to get her hands on some fine necklaces. One, from the 1920s, in wrought silver and set with perfectly cut stones, pleased him particularly.

"Red beryl, banded agate, and topaz," he said.

Rose looked up, surprised. "You know your stones."

His lips twitched upward. "I do," he acknowledged. And although the price for the piece was a bit hefty, he didn't hesitate.

"You aren't from around here, are you?" Rose asked idly as she folded the necklace into a little box, began wrapping it in silvery paper.

"I live in Reno, but I pass through Blake's Folly from time to time. I noticed your shop months ago, and I always promised myself that one day I'd stop in, have a look. This was the perfect occasion: Marina's birthday is on Tuesday."

"You pass through Blake's Folly from time to time? Whatever for?" Rose smirked. "This is the end of the world."

"The world has several ends, and I work in all of them. I'm a geologist."

"Ah, I see. Well, that explains it. That also explains why you knew what the stones in the necklace were." Not that she knew a lot about geology, aside from the fact that it had something—or everything—to do with minerals and lurching over the countryside staring at rocks and measuring things with strange gadgets.

"That explains some of it," he said, taking her in from head to toe with undisguised interest. "If this place is the end of the world, how did you get here?"

"The easiest way possible. I was born here." Rose

glanced out of the window at the early evening light touching up a bleak, empty landscape that would never interest a city slicker, at the gentle snowflakes drifting lazily, as though they had no intention of ever reaching the ground.

"And you stayed?"

He was looking even more curious now—if that were possible. She couldn't blame him. "I did leave Blake's Folly when I was younger. I stayed away for years and was absolutely certain I'd never return, that this place was the absolute pits." She cut a strip of glossy ribbon, curled the ends with her sharp little scissors. "It's funny: there's nothing going on here. The greatest social event of the year is the Blake's Folly Get-Together—and that means awful music, awkward dancing, and gossipmongering. There's no cinema within reasonable distance, no good shopping closer than Reno—and that's a long, boring drive away. Yet, this place has a strange pulling power. So I came back, decided to settle."

"Your husband is from Blake's Folly too?"

Rose's eyes snapped back to his. *Aha*. So, he was still interested and checking out the territory. "No husband."

"An unmarried woman in such an out-of-the-way place?"

What was he asking? If she were lonely? Desperate for male company? Rose laughed outright. "Oh, there are plenty of men around, believe me." There were. They were out on the ranches, or climbing over the hills, or looking for gold, or photographing, or pounding along the history trail, or doing research, or taking care of animals, or looking for fossils, or stopping at the Mizpah Saloon for a drink, a chat, a meal, and a little human warmth out here on the lonely flatland. She'd always had her share of admirers too, although none lived in Blake's Folly—they'd have to be half mad to do something like that. This place was a rusty trailer, scrapyard, abandoned car, clapboard shack, sagging old house community: a dead end if there ever was one.

Now, although he looked amused, he was also slightly abashed. "I think I'm the one who's out of line this time."

Rose grinned. His grin met hers.

He took the pretty gift-wrapped packet she held out, slipped it into the pocket of his leather jacket. Looked out at the night but didn't move away. Why was he hesitating? Because he wanted to stay? Talk to her? Get to know her? Because he too acknowledged the buzz that was still hovering in the air around them, and he wanted to explore it, see where it would go?

Then he turned back to her, the smile still playing around his lips. "Well, I'd better be on my way. Looks like the snow isn't letting up."

"No," Rose agreed. "There have been blizzard warnings all day."

"Yes." His eyes held hers. Warm eyes. Intimate eyes. Eyes that, in certain circumstances, could create havoc with a woman's senses. "Nice talking to you."

"Nice talking to you, too." She meant it.

He still wasn't heading out of the shop. "My name is Jonah. Jonah Livingstone."

"I'm Rose Badger."

"I figured your name might be Rose. This shop is called Second Hand Rose."

"Yes." Her moue was slightly mocking. "Sure, I know it's corny using the title of a song for the name of a shop, but it does get the idea across. And it incites people from elsewhere to stop, take a look."

"I'm living proof of that."

"You are…since Blake's Folly isn't exactly a tourist destination." No, it certainly wasn't. "It isn't even a realistic destination for anyone reasonably sane."

He winked. "I'll keep that in mind." He headed for the door. Finally. "Until next time, Rose."

She waved. "See you then."

He stepped out into the night, turned back, raised his hand in an identical wave. Then vanished into the falling snow and dusky evening.

Next time, he'd said? Rose shrugged. What sort of next time was he referring to? This was Blake's Folly. People always said they'd be back, but they rarely were. Why return to a pile of clapboard shacks and abandoned trailers? This was nowhere. This was the end of the line, socially speaking. This was a has-been. This was home.

****

Meeting Jonah Livingstone had left her with a strangely unsettled feeling. She wondered why, but had no real answer—other than the fact that she'd liked him. Nothing unusual in that, though. Rose loved men, loved talking to them, loved to hear them jawing on about things she would normally never want to think about. She liked their rougher skin, their deeper voices, their broader shoulders. She delighted in making them laugh; she encouraged them. She was good at both of those things, too, and because men knew she liked them, they were happy to open up, confide in her, trust her, be with her.

Sure, that didn't make her a lot of female friends in the world, but having one close woman friend was enough for her—although that particular friend, Alice, was a bit of a crank, a herpetologist who spent all her time studying and rescuing snakes. Alice probably preferred everything slithery, covered with scales, and venomous, to any human being. What could you expect out here? Normal people didn't live in Blake's Folly.

Well…if the place was a washout now, it had been jumpy, raw, and nervous enough back in the old silver boom days. And dangerous. Local legend claimed that back in the late 1800s, no sheriff survived longer than a few months, and that a fair number of cattle rustlers, horse thieves, stagecoach bandits, and bank robbers had once swung from long-vanished gibbets at the town's end. Today's few residents were the descendants of the wild gunslingers and good-time girls, the ones who'd hung around too long, gotten so caught in the gluey languor of this place, they'd been unable to move off.

Jonah. He'd said his name was Jonah. A nice name. Not one you heard often.

Idiot. She was acting like a teenager with a crush on the high school pretty-boy, not like a mature businesswoman. She marched herself into the back room, lifted a soft mauve dress—a perfect 1940s tea gown—from her worktable, slipped it onto a hanger, came back into the shop, and hung the garment in the right place, where it would snag the attention it deserved. Then stood back to admire her handiwork with a smug smile. That dress was a beautiful piece of craftsmanship; the soft fabric glowed, even in the dull light of a snowy winter evening. She knew that, in the next few weeks, some lucky woman would fall in love with it, carry it away, convinced she'd purchased an authentic vintage garment.

It wasn't vintage, of course, but no one had to know. The fabric was right, the style was perfect, the lovely thing was hanging here in her little shop, Second Hand Rose. Anyone could imagine the dress had been worn by some glamorous starlet back in Hollywood's heyday. Even if that wasn't true...Very far from the truth, in fact.

She looked at the large old wooden clock hanging on the wall. Would it matter if she closed up a little early? Of course, it wouldn't. How many customers would be willing to risk the icy roads? None. She didn't feel like sitting down, reading, or scraping together a light dinner, or singing, or drawing, or spending time in her own company. No, she'd go over to the Mizpah Saloon, sit up at the bar, amuse herself, push thoughts of unavailable men like Jonah Livingstone out of her head.

Still...hadn't she loved his coloring, the wonderful crinkles around his mouth, those cheekbones, the eyes that hinted at more exotic genes—perhaps Shoshone? There was something else that drew her too: his aura? His scent?

Come on! Why waste another thought on him? She'd most likely never see the man again.

Slipping into her pink fake fur, she dimmed the shop lights, locked the door, and headed down the treacherously rutted and icy road toward the Mizpah. Time to take her mind off the impossible and do what she did best. Charm everyone. Flirt. Then bask in the admiration of all the men in sight. She'd manage to do all that very well too. All you had to know was how to snag their attention. Then, they'd come snuffling around, all right.

So what if local consensus tagged her as an airhead, an inveterate flirt, and a loose woman no one could take seriously. She didn't mind one bit. Lighthearted flightiness was the image she'd been careful to cultivate over the years here in Blake's Folly; it kept all the bored, nosy gossips in the tiny community satisfied, not prying into her past or her present.

Because one of the things Rose liked best in life was keeping secrets—not that the secrets would have compromised her in any way. They weren't deep, dark things that should best be hidden. No, it was almost a game: hiding who she really was, what she really did. Having a secret life put a tickle into everyday existence, and it kept a sly smile on her lips, nothing more than that.

****

The closer Jonah got to Reno, the worse driving conditions became. Why the hell hadn't he had the sense to stop his journey, spend the night in Blake's Folly? There had been a hotel and bar—the Mizpah Saloon—right in the town's center. He could have taken a room. What difference did it make if he got back home tonight? Marina would be fine without him.

Or would she be? He didn't know, but more often lately, he'd had the feeling that she'd finally realized she didn't really need him, or his support, any longer. If the feeling was right, it was quite a relief.

He'd let her depend on him for too long, and that was far from the deal they had made in the beginning…the deal that stated this situation was a

J. Arlene Culiner

temporary one; that it would end as soon as she felt she was ready to stand on her own two feet, go back to work, take up the thread of her life, become the energetic woman she'd once been.

At which time, he'd be free to live his own life again, to play his beautiful baroque cello for hours on end—that was what he wanted, wasn't it? Or had he become strangely dependent on Marina, taken advantage of the fact that she was in his life, in his apartment? Perhaps he'd been using her as a shield, an excuse to distance himself from others, to protect his independent loner streak. With her there, he couldn't become emotionally involved with anyone else, and he didn't have to make an effort. If that were true, the idea didn't make him any happier. It made him feel like an emotional coward.

His thoughts drifted back to the feisty-looking woman in that colorfully chaotic shop in Blake's Folly: Rose Badger. A funny name. She looked like fun too: a shining woman with an open gaze, a tumble of naturally golden curls, and a ready, good-natured smile. If he'd suggested a drink in the Mizpah Saloon, if he'd invited her out for dinner, would she have accepted? He had the definite feeling she might well have done. Yes, that would have been worth a try. He was pretty certain it would have been an enjoyable evening, too.

But he hadn't done it. He pushed the niggling feeling of regret to the back of his mind as the distant haze of Reno's nightlights glowed pale orange on the horizon.

Chapter Two: Bachelors

On Thursday morning, Rose was working on a sketch when the doorbell tinkled. A customer? She left the back room and went into the shop. Well, well. What a pleasant surprise. Lance Potter, local veterinarian, was standing in the doorway, stamping the snow off his high boots. What was he doing here?

Her heart warmed. "Lance! How nice to see you."

"Rose," he said softly.

Yes, he was pleased to see her too, and that was fine, as far as she was concerned. Lance was a lovely man, and good company. Intelligent. A bachelor. Gorgeous. She did love those laughing eyes of his, the light brown curl of his hair, the mouth that always seemed ready to smile. To share kisses?

She cut the thought short. "What are you doing out this way?"

"Checking some calves out at Roy Palmer's ranch."

"Ah." She smiled. Roy was another one of her admirers; Lance knew that. Did he mind? Rose doubted it. She always had a group of men around her, and she enjoyed their presents of dark chocolate, their invitations to dine out. She also knew that she was merely the catalyst of that particular social group: although ostensibly circling around her, the men—all long-time bachelors—really sought each other's company and relaxed companionship. Rose was fairly certain none of them lost sleep fretting over unrequited love for her.

"Well, do come in, Lance. Take a seat. It's freezing out there. Would you like me to make a cup of coffee to warm you up?"

Lance grinned openly. "Both you and I know you make the worst coffee in Nevada."

"Yes, we do, don't we." Rose grinned back at him. "But not only in Nevada. In the entire west of the United States."

She wasn't in the least bit offended. Everyone who knew her was well aware of her antipathy to cooking, baking, boiling, steaming, mixing, shopping for food, dishwashing, or any other domestic chore. Dusting and sweeping came low on her list too, but she forced herself to do those tasks. She had to keep up a decent image for her customers, also to thwart local tongue-waggers who were ever on the prowl for any old grist to feed their gossip mill. But for her "gentlemen" admirers, her lack of homemaking savvy was part of her appeal: domesticity tended to make confirmed bachelors nervous. Made them fear they'd be hog-tied in no time at all.

"Actually, I can't stay for more than a few minutes."

"You drove all the way into Blake's Folly for a visit of a few minutes?" Her tone was flirtatious, and she could see he liked that.

"I'm afraid so. I'm on my way back to town to take over the clinic. My partner Jeff, who handles the small animal section, is home with the flu, and the waiting room is probably filled with overweight cats and anorexic poodles."

"Or a few neurotic guinea pigs? An armadillo with an identity problem?"

"I can see it all now. Budgies with wisdom teeth and fallen arches." He chuckled in his usual sexy, good-natured way. "Actually, the reason I stopped by was to ask you to dinner. On Friday evening. Are you free?"

"Absolutely. Yes, I'd love to go out to dinner with you."

"How about the Three Penny Inn?"

"Wonderful. I'll get out my glass slippers for the occasion." The Three Penny Inn, with its low lights, plush seats, crisp white tablecloths, and refined food, was a gustatory oasis in the desert—and, naturally, one of her favorite places.

"Good. That's settled." His voice dropped a few tones, sounded rich, thrilling. "I'm looking forward to it."

"So am I." She meant it too.

Lance wound his woolen scarf more tightly around his neck, pulled on his leather gloves. "See you Friday, then. At around seven? I'll pick you up."

"Do you want to drive all the way out here? It's so far from where you live. I can meet you halfway, if you'd like. That would be no problem for me."

"For *me*, it would be a problem." His eyes were warm, but his expression was determined. "I'd like you to think I'm a gentleman."

She glimmered up at him. "I wasn't in the least bit worried that you weren't."

He hesitated. Then stepped closer to her, bent, brushed her lips in a brief kiss. A kiss that was halfway between friendship and desire. A kiss that promised more.

Then he was gone, crossing the lane and climbing into his jeep. Rose felt extremely satisfied. Dinner with Lance on Friday evening. What fun that was going to be.

Of course, she'd known Lance for quite a while now. He often stopped by to visit her when he was in the area, to invite her to the Mizpah Saloon for a drink and amusing conversation. Until recently, his serious lady friend had been Suzie, a lawyer in Reno. Now, he and Suzie were no longer together—something that wouldn't upset Lance, Rose knew. He'd always made it clear he was the sort of man who went from one relationship to another, that any emotional involvement had a time limit on it—a limit quickly reached when a woman mentioned permanence, new kitchenware, moving in together, babies, or joint bank accounts.

And now, free again, he seemed to have set his sights on Rose. Which was fine with her. An affair with Lance? Why not? It might be fun. On the other hand, would it be in her best interests? She did like Lance, and she didn't want permanence either—she'd had that once, and once was quite enough. These days, she preferred her freedom.

Did that mean she would always feel that way? Who knew? Live for the moment, that was her motto. She enjoyed her own company. What she wanted from men was that first zing of romance, the first flirt, and all the electricity of getting to know someone of the opposite sex. She had no patience for the flat lack of excitement that chugged in on the heels of permanence, the minor irritations that colored the daily menu of any long-term relationship.

If that made her a bad person in some people's eyes, well, she didn't care one bit. Life was for fun, she'd decided that long ago, and no righteous moralist was going to ruin her round on the carousel. As far as an affair with Lance went…how would it feel knowing she was one more pretty flower on an endlessly long daisy chain?

Not that she had to worry about where their relationship might go. Not yet, anyway. She and Lance were at the very beginning of a more personal relationship: the courtship stage; the testing stage; the getting-to-know-each-other-for-a-possible-romance stage. They were taking it slowly, and that was fine with her. It kept things in suspense, exciting. This, as far as she was concerned, was the best part.

****

The Mizpah Saloon, Hotel, and Restaurant, a relic left over from the old days, was a landmark of sorts. Time hadn't altered its facade, nor the large balcony with wrought-iron railing running along the front of the building, nor the grand terrace below, nor the old-fashioned sash windows on the upper floors. Sagging, usually neglected, sometimes cherished and coddled—it all depended on the owner of the moment—this building was the pride and joy of Blake's Folly. It was witness to the fact that this had been a town of some importance…way back when.

Nonetheless, you had to be a local to love the Mizpah, Rose reflected as she pushed open the wide door at lunchtime. Here, despite the shiny brass footrails, gleaming mirrors, and bad Western paintings on the walls, the leather seats were cracked and tables deeply scratched. This was also the home-sweet-home of all of Blake's Folly's losers—and there were quite a few of those. You probably had to be a local to *want* to go in there—especially today—because Sly Grimes, lead singer and guitarist of the Old Boy's Band, had decided this was the right time for an impromptu country music concert.

Sly, ambitious but tone deaf, loved the musical scale's high notes yet rarely reached them. He relished twanging his guitar, although he hadn't perfected more than four chords. He thought of himself as a poet, a creator of brilliant lyrics, even if his songs rarely consisted of more than two, constantly repeated sentences. Still, Sly and his Old Boy's Band was the closest thing Blake's Folly had to stardom, even if stardom meant that all fifty-odd residents of the community had heard of them and, worse still, had heard them play. Knowing local taste, all probably thought the band was pretty good, too.

Rose, not one of the enamored fans, grimaced when she heard the racket. She should have stayed home in her cozy work room and found something simple to nibble on. Now, it was too late to turn around, sneak back out. Jane Grimes, fond mother of Sly, had caught sight of her and was waving wildly, motioning Rose over to the barstool next to her own.

"What yuh havin' ta drink, Rose? I'm buying."

Of course she was. Jane needed witnesses to her son's genius. As her son's unequivocal supporter and main cheerleader, Jane dressed the part: fluorescent togs, dyed orange hair, wild pink lipstick, and thick black eyeliner that would have done justice to any neophyte who hadn't quite gotten the hang of a steady hand. Inwardly, Rose sighed: she knew she was doomed, condemned to listen to a boastful mother's tribute. With resignation, she ordered a coffee.

"Sly wanted to comm-oo-nicate with the cree-aytive muse today," Jane said, when Rose was comfortably ensconced on the stool beside hers. "Say-ed he has a few nyew tunes he wants to have ready for the Get-Together."

"Yes, the Old Boy's Band will be playing again, I imagine." What was there to imagine? The Old Boy's Band always played at the Get-Together. They were always awful.

"Course, they will. The Get-Together wouldn't be the same without them."

"No. It wouldn't." Rose suppressed the wild giggle forming deep in her belly. Still, no denying the Get-Together was the biggest social event in Blake's Folly, although any sane outsider would give it a wide berth. She couldn't blame them.

This place, almost classified as a ghost town, was too far off the beaten track to interest the ever-popular ghost-town bus tours, and carloads of tourists armed with cameras rarely showed up. Why would they? In warmer weather, the vegetation was sparse. No trees, no hedges, no lawns, no greenery, but a lot of dust, and a great many treacherous, highly unpleasant spiky shrubs with colorful local names: Granny-Clutch-Me, Hound's Snaggle, Poisonous Snake Treat.

To make up for all that was lacking—a school, a cinema, streetlights, employment, infrastructure, sidewalks, a library, paved roads—the community created bake-ups, garage sales, group birthday celebrations, and party nights such as the yearly Get-Together. These events, although kitschy and down-home, were well-attended by the eccentric locals who were nosy enough to meet with great frequency—in case there was any new gossip to chew over.

"Glad my boy come back to me again after livin' the wild life in the dirty ole big city."

Wild life? Sly? Really? The giggle made itself felt again, tickling, fighting to be released, and Rose bit her lip. She knew that, some years earlier, Sly had desperately tried to become a successful musician in San Francisco's nightclubs, and, although the competition was rarely superior, he had failed to make his mark. But wild life? No way. Sly was too sweet-tempered and naïve for recklessness.

At that moment, Sly hit one of his well-worn four chords, followed it up with one of his own compositions:

Gonna miss my babe,
If she goes
Gonna miss the babe
Yes, I will…
Gonna miss her, miss her, miss her
If she goes

"That song Sly's playing now?" Jane shouted above the racket. "It's brand new. He's preparing it special for the event."

"Oh, really?" Rose tried to look impressed, but it was under great duress. To her ears, the noise sounded like an underwater dirge on a sunken ship, not a love song.

"People come from all over to hear the Old Boy's Band," said Jane. "They got lotsa followers. Even young kids come to listen to them, although two of the boys are pushin' sixty."

"Ah." Remaining laconic seemed the best solution. Did the band really have followers? Really? Well, living miles from anywhere decent could certainly drive people to take desperate measures. Perhaps Jane mistook the people who showed up regularly at the Mizpah for followers.

"Too bad you don't wanna participate no more." Jane looked both arch and chastising at the same time.

Rose peered at her. What was the woman on about now? "Participate? I always participate. I'm here at the Get-Together every single year, hell or high water. Neither snow, nor rain, nor heat, nor gloom of night, would stay me from my local duty."

"I don't mean in that way." Looking mighty cunning now, Jane leaned in closer. "I mean joining Sly, like."

"Joining Sly?" Rose had no idea where this conversation was headed, although she did have the sharp, sneaking suspicion that the direction wasn't one she wanted to take.

"Used to sing a lot when you was a young girl."

"Yes, well…"

"Your granny taught you. She had a fine voice. Your mother did too, but she wasted it like she wasted all the good things the Lord give her."

Hoping to bring the conversation to an end, even if it meant leaving without lunch, Rose slugged back her tepid coffee, slid off her barstool, and shrugged herself into her pink coat. "Sorry, Jane, I have to get back to the shop in case a customer comes by. Thanks for the drink. Next time, the round's on me."

But, no, that nosy woman couldn't be fobbed off so easily, not when she had a tasty morsel of information

21

in her hands and wanted to see if it would glean her a nibble. "Sly told me you used to sing professional. Said he seen you, too, once."

"That was back then," Rose said testily.

"That's what I'm saying. You had talent, girl. You shouldn't never let talent go to waste."

This was definitely a conversation that had to end. Because the thought of singing with the Old Boy's Band was so totally nightmarish (if it hadn't been so funny), also because the subject of singing was one she definitely had no intention of pursuing. It was taboo. It was one of her many deep secrets.

****

After returning to the shop, she worked nonstop throughout the afternoon, inspired by the soft flowing fabric on her worktable in the back room. By dusk, she had designed and cut out what would be, when sewn together by her seamstresses Ana or Tereza, a lovely 1930s cocktail dress with a bias-cut skirt and keyhole neckline. An authentic vintage dress.

Well…it would *look* like an authentic vintage dress, even though it was new—that was all part of the secret. People never asked the right questions. "Is this a real vintage dress?" would, of course, get the answer, "yes." Few people actually asked: "Was this vintage dress actually made in the 1930s?" If they did, she would have explained that it would have been stylish in the '30s, but that it was a new creation.

Perhaps people didn't want to know the truth. Perhaps they wanted to believe they had made an expedition to the state of Nevada and found a rare treasure in Rose's unconventional secondhand clothing shop. Or that they had found a gem via the Internet.

What did it matter? Rose knew her styles were authentic, that the fabrics were top quality, and that the skill of her seamstresses was incomparable. So why would anyone complain?

She had been so intent on her work, she hadn't noticed that the outside light had waned, that night had pulled in. Only when she heard the jangle of the bell above the shop door, did she glance up at the clock. Six forty-five in the evening? How time had flown. A customer this late on a cold winter's day? She should have locked up by now. Perhaps it was one of her admirers who had come calling. Which one? Brad Mace, the rancher? He'd been hinting lately that he might like to make a bid to win her favor and spend more time in her company. Or Roy Palmer. If Roy and Brad didn't both think that the latest cattle news was the most fascinating subject around, she might have encouraged them.

Smoothing her soft red sweater over her hips, she left the workroom, headed into the shop. Stopped dead. That smile, the craggy face, the wonderful brown eyes. Her heart thrilled. He was back. Jonah Livingstone.

Still having the same effect on her, too. He'd said he'd be back, hadn't he? Well, yes…but she hadn't believed him. Yet, here he was. Because he'd been that interested? She couldn't push down the pleasure she felt at seeing him again, although she did her best to quash it, to be less enthusiastic. To stop her heart from thumping a little faster.

Surely, he wasn't here for her. He was probably here to buy Marina, that woman he lived with, another bit of vintage jewelry. Probably. Unless, worse yet, he wanted to return the one he'd bought last time.

23

She smiled at him. "Don't tell me you can't keep away from Blake's Folly."

He smiled back. "You did say the place had a strange pulling power."

He actually remembered what she'd said? Incredible. What was going on here? She cocked an eyebrow, tried to act casual. "What can I help you with today?"

"Nothing, actually." He hesitated. "I was passing by Blake's Folly on my way back to Reno, and I remembered seeing the Mizpah Saloon and Hotel the other night."

"That's right," said Rose warily. What was he going to propose? A roll in the hay? Surely not. He didn't seem like a coarse man. "It isn't a hotel anymore—except for ghosts and spiders—since the upstairs rooms haven't been dusted for at least a half century. Nowadays, it's simply a bar and restaurant. But it is the center of life in Blake's Folly."

"Is the food any good?"

"Well…let's say it's…uh…simple. The cook's inventiveness stops at an excellent cheese plate, or homemade sandwiches and freshly cut fries—real ones, not frozen, not reconstituted—as improbable as that sounds in today's modern world. There are other things too, of course, but I'd stick with the cheese, the fries, or the sandwiches. The toasted cheese and tomato sandwiches are the best I've ever tasted, mainly because the cheese is the real thing, thick slices carved from a huge block." She stopped, laughed at herself. "Listen to me rattling on as though a tomato and cheese sandwich is an original gourmet recommendation."

"Sounds fine to me. Would you accept an

invitation to have dinner with me there?"

"Dinner?" Rose stared at him as if dinner were a concept she'd never before considered.

"Yes, I know." He looked rueful. "From what you've told me, it's not a glamorous invitation. I doubt there are candles and tablecloths. However, it is almost seven o'clock. I'd like to eat something before hitting the road again and heading back to Reno. If you haven't had your dinner yet, I'd love it if you joined me."

Rose slid him a cautious look from under her lashes. What sort of invitation was this? Hadn't he made it clear that he was an attached man? "Do you think your, uh…" She searched for the right word: lady friend? Fiancée? Mistress? Squeeze? Paramour? She opted for caution. "Your housemate…would approve?"

He threw back his head and laughed heartily. "I have breakfast, lunch, and dinner, with many people— men and women—every day of the week. My friends include both men and women. Do you think I have to call Marina and ask permission to meet with them?"

She smiled back. "Point taken."

"And your answer?"

"I accept."

So. This plainly wasn't an attempted seduction. That was fine. Things were clear. He was in a solid relationship. What he was going to have with her would be a casual friendship. But—yes, she had to admit it— she was disappointed that things had to be that way.

Chapter Three: At the Mizpah Saloon

He helped her into her warm coat—a fluffy, pale pink, fake fur Marina wouldn't be caught dead wearing—and waited while she locked the door to her shop.

"Where do you live?"

"Right here." One mitten-covered hand patted the wooden doorpost.

"In the shop?"

"Not exactly. The shop is in the front room. This place is a lot bigger than it looks, and there are quite a few other rooms in the back. The building dates from the 1870s when it housed a local newspaper, the *Morning Sun*."

He searched up and down the deserted road. There were no lights twinkling in any of the surrounding buildings, and most looked as though they'd been empty for many long years. It seemed a lonely, isolated place for a woman living on her own, but why mention it? What did he know about Rose Badger? Nothing.

"Well, at least there are no parking problems here in town. Come, my van's over there." He gestured to the space between two wooden shacks where he'd parked the green jeep with the logo of the University of Nevada Geographic Survey on its side. "It's not a glitzy vehicle, but I've been out surveying at the Winterback Mine."

She stared. "You want to drive to the Mizpah?"

"Why? Do you want to walk there?"

"Why drive such a short distance? It's two streets away."

She was right. It would be silly to drive, but he knew that Marina would have insisted on the car, complaining that the snow would ruin her shoes, the wind would mess her hair, that it was too cold, that she'd break her neck on the rough, barely-paved back road. Why was he comparing the two women? Marina and Rose Badger were as different as chalk and cheese. Why think of Marina now? Why ruin the time he was spending with this tiny, sparkling woman who walked beside him with definite, springing steps?

He liked the way she watched him, tilting her head slightly before answering a question, letting the glacial light of the moon caress her high, flat cheekbones. It was odd: he didn't know Rose Badger at all, but there had been an instant recognition when he'd first caught sight of her. Or had it been an immediate attraction? One he hadn't been able to forget.

He hadn't quite told the truth when he'd said he'd been passing by. He'd been on another route altogether, and heading for Blake's Folly meant making quite a detour. For what? For a one-off meeting with this charming and lovely woman whose presence seemed to brighten the dark with a translucent light; for a casual dinner and some getting-to-know-you conversation before driving back to Reno.

"Tell me. Was your mother thinking of a desert rose flower when she named you?"

Rose's laughter was a tinkle in the icy air. "My mother thinking of flowers? No way she had botany in mind when it came to me. No, she was more into your line: geology."

"Geology?"

She nodded. "Selenite gypsum or rose rock. She and my father left Nevada to go honeymoon in Oklahoma. That's where she saw her first desert roses, and that's where I was conceived. Nine months later, she was still so cross at getting pregnant and having a baby, she took revenge by naming me after a crystal cluster."

He chuckled. "I hope she didn't hold the grudge for too long."

"Oh, but she did." Rose nodded. "She's always thought she was programmed for better things than domesticity and motherhood. Since she was eighteen years old back then, she was certain that a glitzy life was in store for her."

"What sort of glitzy life?"

"She didn't have the foggiest idea, really. When she dropped out of school, people told her to go to Reno, use her wonderful singing voice to find work. But she was lazy. Instead of actually going for what she wanted, she settled for waitressing over at the Dew Drop Inn, fifteen miles from here. One day, my father sashayed in, told her he was a Hollywood talent scout, then declared his passion. That convinced her Lady Luck was smiling, and escape through marriage was the best solution."

"It wasn't?"

"What sort of escape could she hope for? My father was an inveterate liar. He had no contacts, and he'd never been anywhere near Hollywood. As for my mother, she thought that some big-time record producer would strut into one of the lowlife Reno bars she hung around in, hear her sing, decide she was star material, and cart her off to fairyland."

"Your parents stayed together?"

"For a while. My father lived on the pipe dream of getting rich mining silver, and he never had a cent to his name. My mother continued waiting tables to keep us all in chow. Eventually, my father ran off with Nelly Hatchet who was years younger and had money in the bank, and my mother began working her way through all the available deadbeats in Reno before coming back here and hooking up with Alf Paltry."

"She's still in Blake's Folly?"

"Right over that rise on the horizon." Her hand waved toward a destination that was completely indefinable in the dark. "In a beat-up trailer, chain-smoking and drinking herself to death with Alf." She looked up at him, her eyes somber. "I did tell you this is the end of the world. And right now, we're about to enter the Mizpah, a former den of iniquity. I hope you're prepared."

"Sounds fascinating." It did.

"You think so? I might tell you some of the old stories one day. They aren't terribly pretty."

The warning sounded dire enough, but when he glanced down at her, he noticed that her eyes were sparkling with humor.

****

"Looks like this place hasn't changed much in the last hundred years."

"It hasn't. Neither have the clients." Rose surveyed the pithy-looking men, the rough-looking women, all of them standing up at the bar; yes, they probably resembled the Mizpah's original customers. "Of course, their costumes are different. I mean, can anyone imagine pioneers, cattle rustlers, gunslingers, saloon ladies, and miners wearing worn jogging pants and sagging sports shoes?"

His laughter was a gratifying sound.

"Of course, the local manners have changed too," she continued. "Fortunately. Back in the gold mining days, this was quite the place for deadly shoot-outs. And since law and order wasn't a concept understood by everyone, masked vigilantes had to step in."

"How did they calm local tempers?"

"Since their arguments included a rope, they convinced quite a few bad boys that Blake's Folly was no place for them."

All the barflies turned, gawked suspiciously at Jonah, a stranger in these parts, but that was normal behavior in small out-of-the-way places. She smiled, greeted everyone, and soon the grunting, low-browed primeval mistrust was replaced by undiluted nosiness.

She headed for a corner booth where there was enough distance for a private conversation, although she knew everyone would soon be inching in closer, straining to hear every word she and Jonah exchanged. Ned Stalks, the owner, ambled over as soon as they sat down—ostensibly, to find out what they were drinking, but really to get a closer look at Jonah. Typical Blake's Folly prying.

"You folks wanna order something?"

Rose winced at Ned's definitely un-classy, typical Blake's Folly style. Then again, she *had* cautioned Jonah. "We're here for dinner."

Ned scratched his chin. "Cook's in a bad mood.

Won't get anything decent tonight. That's a warning."

Rose knew perfectly well that the cook in question, Trix, was Ned's cactus-tongued wife. Jonah wouldn't know that, of course. She didn't dare look over at him, certain if she did, she'd burst out laughing. Since he wasn't familiar with the usual cranky Blake's Folly manners, he must be feeling completely confused, out-of-place. "How about a toasted tomato and cheese sandwich with fries, Ned? You think Trix will run to that?"

"Might."

Rose looked questioningly at Jonah. No, he didn't seem at all confused. The corners of his mouth were twitching; he was also fighting down laughter. However, he did manage to say, "I'll have the same as Rose, please."

Ned shrugged, began to shuffle off, before suddenly turning again. "You folks drinking anything?"

Jonah looked at Rose. She smiled. "Ned keeps an excellent California Cabernet Sauvignon."

"Then we'll have a bottle."

When Ned had disappeared into the kitchen, Rose leaned across the table. "Don't pay attention to his rudeness. This is a community of cranks, and Ned is one of the more reasonable ones. Believe it or not, Ned is actually a wine snob. He won't tolerate plonk on his premises, despite the local preference for cheap booze in vast quantities."

"Living here is beginning to sound like fun."

"You have to be in a good mood," Rose said somberly. But she was enjoying herself, she really was. She adored men who smiled, laughed, and had a sense of humor. They weren't that thick on the ground—at

31

least, in Blake's Folly, they weren't thick on the ground.

Ned appeared with two long-stemmed glasses and a dusty bottle of wine: his wine bottles were always dusty, as if they came from some deep and ancient subterranean network of cellars. Rose suspected, however, that he'd watched too many wine connoisseur programs on television and was copying all he'd seen to hoist up the image of this end-of-the-road hostelry. Deftly, Ned uncorked the bottle, sniffed the cork. Then, like the perfect sommelier in a five-star glamour eatery, poured a little into Jonah's glass.

Jonah's eyes were twinkling. He'd obviously understood the game and was willing to play along. Picking up his glass, he sniffed the wine, swirled it around for a few seconds, and then sipped. "Very nice."

Evidently chuffed, Ned poured out a glass for Rose, completed Jonah's, then left them—probably temporarily—in peace.

Rose sipped. "Delicious. As I said…"

Jonah nodded. "I'm impressed."

"Impressed?"

"I feel like I've accidentally stumbled into a secret world of sorts. A hidden corner of the desert that no one has discovered yet."

"No one normal, you mean." But pleased she could show him something halfway nice in this backwoods nowhere of a place, she relaxed, leaned back in her seat. "So tell me all about being a geologist. I've never met one before. What do you do? You don't spend all your time wandering around the desert staring at rocks, do you?"

"That sounds pretty boring, even to me."

The way his eyes crinkled at the corners when he smiled took her breath away. He was...lovely to look at. She smiled back at him. "To me too. I was getting worried."

"Actually, our primary job is studying earth history—in particular, climate change and threats to the environment. We also try to offer solutions to flooding and pollution. My own specialty, paleontology, explores the history of life on earth. I've always wanted to know how the world evolved."

"Who do geologists work for?"

"Some of us work for natural resource companies, or consulting companies, or government agencies, or non-profit organizations. I've never worked in the private sector, because I prefer academia, using my experience in the field to teach others."

"*Doctor* Livingstone, I presume?"

He smiled again, and all those lovely crinkles around his eyes returned. "Yes, I'm another Dr. Livingstone. And being attached to the university allows me to do fieldwork. That's what I enjoy the most."

"Here in Nevada?"

Jonah leaned forward in his seat, and Rose could feel his enthusiasm: he was definitely a man who loved his work, perhaps as much as she loved hers. "You can't imagine how rich the invertebrate and vertebrate fossil life is in this state."

"Tell me about it."

He hesitated, although his eyes sparkled hopefully. "Are you sure you want to know? I can get pretty carried away, and you might be bored."

"Test me. Actually, I love learning about stuff I

don't know. And you aren't a boring man. I've known you for less than an hour, but I think your enthusiasm could carry away whole crowds."

He acknowledged the compliment but didn't look entirely convinced. "Well, let me know when you start to fall asleep."

"Promise." No, he could never bore her, she knew that instinctively. She longed to touch him, reach out, trace the knuckles of his hand with one finger, feel his warmth. It was crazy to be so attracted, but he was wonderfully seductive. And his mouth was fine, sexy. His dedication, his earnest smile were so endearing.

"Well…to begin with, both eastern and southern Nevada were once covered by a warm shallow sea filled with reefs, mollusks, and ammonites. There were ichthyosaurs, too."

"Ichthyosaurs?"

"Large marine lizards. Fascinating creatures. They appeared around 250 million years ago, evolving from a group of unidentified land reptiles that returned to the sea, like the ancestors of modern-day dolphins and whales."

"Why? Why did that happen?"

"To adapt to changing climatic conditions."

"Where do you get this information? Not from fossils."

"You'd be surprised how much fossils reveal. One ichthyosaur fossil showed that, while the creature had been hunting ammonites, it was ambushed by a pliosaurid that severed its tail."

"And then?"

"The ichthyosaur drowned, sank to the bottom, and eventually became fossilized."

"What in heaven's name is a pliosaurid?"

"Short-necked cousins of modern turtles with massive toothed jaws."

He talked of the fossil footprints belonging to the camels, horses, lions, wolves, mammoths, and giant ground sloths that once lived here and made that different, long-vanished world come alive. She'd seen fossils before in her life, of course—hadn't everybody?—and she'd never given them a second thought. But the passionate flame in his eyes was touching—although, no denying it, fossils, rocks with unexplained whorls, were far from her world of fabrics and further from her secret passion for music.

"I promise you, I'll never look at a fossil in the same way again," she said. "Not that I'd recognize a fossil footprint or an ammonite, of course."

"I could show you the difference, if you'd like…if you're really interested, that is."

"I am," she said sincerely. "I'd like to read my environment more efficiently. And I'd really like to see some of the things you've discovered."

"You mean that?"

His surprise seemed so sincere, she wondered if Marina, the woman he lived with, thought paleontology, geology, and fossils were a bore, or at least too dusty for her designer togs. "Of course I do. I wouldn't have said so otherwise. I'm not all that polite."

He watched her silently. Then nodded. "Okay. I'll take you out to a field site one day."

"Will you really?"

"Yes, ma'am. I wouldn't have said so otherwise. I'm not all that polite either."

"Touché." Rose laughed.

His laughter joined hers. Their eyes met, a secret glance, one full of promise, somehow, although promises were impossible. There was another woman in the picture.

That wasn't the only reason nothing would ever happen, Rose thought. There was one other big, devastating reason: the difference in their education. Like her mother, she had never finished high school. Jonah was a professor. He was way out of her league. He really did come from quite another section of the Milky Way.

****

Outside the Mizpah, deep dark enfolded them, but the frost-covered ground sparkled like a million diamonds. Despite the bone-chilling cold, the night seemed to contain a thick, magical quality—unless the magic was the vivacious energy this glowing woman beside him exuded.

Content, relaxed, Jonah breathed in the dry, dust-laden air he needed, that he considered essential to his well-being. His love for the bleakness of this area with its flat beige landscape, its dun green vegetation, its mysterious harshness, had been one reason he had become a geologist. If some thought the desert austere, he knew of the rarely seen wealth that lay deep in the ground. Above ground, he'd been in the privileged position to see mule deer, bobcats, mountain beaver, spotted bats, desert tortoises, sidewinders, rattlers, chukar partridges, and little gray lizards: he respected them all.

There was no one else in the quiet streets as they headed back to Second Hand Rose, and the few teetering dwellings were dark shapes against the starry sky.

"I don't see any lights. Are all these buildings abandoned?"

"Most of them, yes." She stopped walking, looked around her, as if examining the empty landscape for the first time. "Believe it or not, we're now standing on Main Street. Once upon a time, in this town's bustling heyday during the silver boom, there were three mercantile stores, a bank, an assay office, an opera house, meat markets, a laundry, a blacksmith, a post office, a rather grand hotel, a courthouse and jail, and some twenty saloons."

"Where did the town's water come from?"

"At first, it was hauled in by mule teams. Later, when this became a boomtown, the mining companies piped it in. Today, all residents know it's a precious commodity, so we keep as much rain water captured in tanks as we can, like in the old days." She stopped walking, pointed. "Behind that huge pile of rocks, there was a bootlegger's still during prohibition. Beside that was the town's last but most famous brothel."

"In that empty lot?"

"It burnt down long before I was born. Of course, as far as brothels went, back in the 1800s, there were quite a few here in town. Blake's Folly was known for them. The hot red star in the desert, people used to call the place. The men—and the girls who worked in the brothels—flocked in."

He nodded thoughtfully. "Back in the days when people had money to spend. When ore could be worth as much as $150 a ton."

"Absolutely." She nodded. "With three mining

companies in Blake's Folly, there was a lot of money around. We were on the railway line to Reno, but the glory didn't last long. There was the recession of 1908, and then people discovered that the ore deposits weren't as extensive as everyone had believed. Soon, the mines were running empty, and the railway tracks were ripped out. By the 1920s, any person sane enough to do so had pulled up stakes, left town, headed for livelier places."

"Except for those who didn't mind the idea of living in a semi-ghost town."

"Exactly."

"Your family stayed?"

In the dark, he could see the cynical twist to her mouth. "I did say that all the sane folks left."

Amused, he challenged: "You're still here too."

"The madness is hereditary, obviously." She sighed. "Yet, I can't imagine going to live anywhere else now. There's something about the air, something special about living here. In a strange way I can't begin to explain, I feel as though it's a privilege to be in Blake's Folly. I believe, sometimes, that these streets are filled with ghosts, and that all the original inhabitants are still here, watching, making sure we keep the town in existence."

"That gives you the feeling of being in a haven."

She gazed up at him, eyes wide. "How did you know that? You're right, of course. Out there, in the big wide world, there's chaos, madness, and continual noise—sirens, traffic, the roar of industry. Here, there's silence and peace. Except…" She grimaced. "Except when our local musicians, the guys in the Old Boy's Band, decide it's the right moment for a concert."

He guffawed. "That bad, are they?"

"Worse. In the old days, local miners got together and formed a brass band. I've heard it was a pretty ghastly, noisy affair, but I'll bet they sounded like a symphony orchestra compared to the Old Boys. Okay…so outside of local unmelodiousness, this is a peaceful place."

"Peaceful? That could be an illusion. Sometimes the big mad world intrudes on small places."

As soon as the words were out of his mouth, he felt like kicking himself. Why introduce his cynical doubts? Perhaps because he had seen too many signs of violence out in the areas he crossed in the flatland: the ubiquitous bullet holes and empty cartridges; the burnt-out cars; the scattered clothes and stolen, abandoned suitcases; the heaps of plastic and rubbish left behind by campers and weekend visitors; the tin cans and rusting barbecue grills; the wooden benches and picnic tables hacked to bits for firewood; the animal corpses. He also knew of the danger posed by the unrestricted sale of handguns, rifles, shotguns, and machine guns.

She didn't deny the truth of his words. "Yes. That's true enough. But no matter where we are, we all have to live with the knowledge that bad things might happen. So we choose to focus on the good."

A wise woman, he thought. A surprising woman. Her knowledge of this town she lived in was also unexpected. So was her eagerness, her bright intelligence. He knew he was attracted by far more than her evident beauty. The thought filled his heart with warmth. And a rare feeling of hope.

Chapter Four: Lance

Jonah sat in his office in the geology department of the university, well aware that he was being anything but efficient. He should have gone back out to the Winterback Mine, joined the rest of the team, done some surveying, been useful. After that? Perhaps stop in Blake's Folly on the way back. Again? That could get to be a habit. An agreeable habit.

He thought about Rose Badger, of the evening in her company, of their conversation. What had she done to him? Bewitched him? Her image had stayed with him throughout the night, those beautifully drawn features, the lively twinkle in her slightly slanted pale blue eyes. She wasn't a classic beauty in the beauty contest sense, but she sparkled with life, and the warmth of her smile dazzled.

Had he bored her with his talk of fossils, of vanished eras? He didn't think so. She really had seemed genuinely interested in all he'd said. Then again, she was the sort of woman who made men feel good. Sexy, beautiful, attentive, and alert: what man could resist all that?

He'd had to refuse her lure, although last night he'd wanted nothing more than to know her better, pull her into his arms, feel her lips. And that, for the moment, was out of the question.

Sure, having dinner with a woman other than

Marina was an everyday occurrence. In his work, he met many intelligent attractive women, and he enjoyed their company. It was his reaction to Rose, the deep instant attraction he'd felt, that made all the difference. But the fact that Marina was still living in his apartment made him feel like a dirty old man or an errant husband, although both those categories were far from the truth.

So what was he? A man who had willingly put himself in an impossible situation and had stayed there? Why? Because he liked the image of himself as a white knight, a do-gooder? Because he was afraid of hurting Marina? Of course, she knew they had no future together, that this situation had never been a permanent one; wasn't that why she had recently become more dependent, more demanding?

He couldn't blame her. He was the one at fault. For letting himself believe he could protect Marina from herself; for letting things drift; for hoping she'd put her failed relationship with that con man, Matt Wilton, behind her.

How long would he continue on like this? It had already been too long. Sitting with Rose last night had changed things radically; knowing she was out there was reason enough to take control of his life. Okay. Until Marina cut back on the tranquilizers and got back to work, he wasn't a free man. In the meantime, he had to make sure that Rose didn't forget him. In case…in case something special developed between them. A deep friendship? A love story? Who knew? He certainly didn't. Not yet.

****

"So there Barry was, in Frankfurt, in a city he didn't know. He couldn't speak the language, he

J. Arlene Culiner

couldn't remember the name of his hotel, he had no idea what street it was on. On top of that, he was jet-lagged but had spent the evening roving from bar to bar, soaking up German beer. By now, it was late. All he wanted was a bed, so he wandered around the streets, thinking he'd find his hotel eventually. He didn't. Then, he got into a taxi because he found a driver who spoke English—and he asked him to cruise the area. Barry was sure he'd recognize the hotel when he saw it, or that its name would ring a bell. So, round and round they drove, but no luck." Lance paused, his white teeth flashing.

"And?" Rose leaned forward, ready for the punch line.

"That was it. He couldn't find it."

"How awful."

"Well, at least he had all his papers on him— passport, plane ticket, money. So, he decided to take a room in another hotel, sleep, go look again in the morning."

"Then what happened?"

"He never found the first hotel, although he kept searching. A few days later he flew back home, to Reno." Lance's grin broadened.

"What an amazing story." It was amusing too…sort of. "Poor man." She was feeling sorry for the guy, lost in a city he didn't know. All his belongings— the new suitcase he'd bought for the trip, the new clothes—safely locked away in a hotel he would never find again.

Lance seemed entertained by his friend's plight. "He's never traveled out of the country since."

"I can understand why." She waited for his show of

empathy—which didn't come. "Don't you feel sorry for him?"

"Hell, no. I've known Barry all my life. He's a mad scientist type, quite brilliant too, yet he's constantly getting himself into situations like that."

She leaned back into the comfortable red velvet armchair as Lance ordered a second round of drinks for the two of them, wine for her, something non-alcoholic for himself. That was Lance, all right: he was driving, and he was a responsible man. As a veterinarian whose practice meant he covered countless miles every day, he would never take risks. He would never put her at risk, either. A nice man. A most engaging admirer. Utterly gorgeous. Hollywood gorgeous, with those sculptured features and long fingers, that lean, muscular body. Now she also knew he was definitely courting her. Which was flattering. Exciting too…wasn't it? Well…it should have been exciting. Somehow, it wasn't as exciting as she'd thought it might be.

Normally, she'd be thrilled to be here, dressed up to the nines and sitting pretty in the calm, rarefied atmosphere of the Three Penny Inn, one of the nicest restaurants in the vicinity. She knew the food would be wonderfully delicious, that Lance would do his best to captivate her. But, somehow, some of the hoped-for glitter was absent. Or was it Lance's appeal that had dimmed?

Why? Oh yes, she knew perfectly well what the answer to that was. Lance Potter had been overshadowed by someone else: Jonah Livingstone. *Now, if that doesn't make me a fickle creature, what does?* She also knew how stupid she was being. Jonah Livingstone was sharing an apartment with a woman.

He was buying presents for her. He was out-of-bounds. Yet, despite her best efforts to push him out of her mind, her thoughts kept returning to his smile, the sound of his voice, his broad shoulders, the shine of his hair, his laughter, and his conversation.

And all her daydreams had an "if only" prefix.

Dreaming of the university professor, are you? She was. *You must be nuts.* She mentally kicked herself for her foolish thoughts. *Forget about the guy.* If he were free, someone like Jonah might see her as a good-time girl, an easy roll in the hay, not as a potential partner. For serious relationships, he'd stick to people of his own educational or professional level. *Get on with your own life. Don't waste your time.*

Perhaps that was why she found Jonah so alluring. He was unavailable. She could never win or refuse him. She would never have to run the risk of a relationship with him or be disappointed when it didn't work out. He would always be a fantasy, and that was far better than reality.

"The party is on Saturday night," Lance was saying. "Are you free?"

"Saturday?" Rose pulled herself back into the present, to this dinner with Lance. What had he asked her? To go someplace with him? She didn't have the foggiest idea where, but she knew the answer to his question: "You know I'm rarely—if ever—free on Saturdays."

Lance's eyes flashed but not with hostility. With amusement. He was smiling too—a rueful smile. "No, you don't seem to be."

Rose smiled back at him. "No, I don't, do I."

"Your secret Saturdays."

"Exactly."

"You won't tell me what you get up to, either."

She tilted her head back, broadened her smile into a wide Cheshire cat grin, one that men found irresistible. One that softened any refusal and took the sting out of rejection. "No. I'm not. Isn't that what deep secrets are all about?"

Lance arched one wonderful eyebrow. "No one knows what the secret is?"

"No one," she confirmed. It was untrue, of course, because there were a few hundred people who knew exactly what she got up to. But not her friends, her admirers, her neighbors, her mother, or her customers. There was nothing as delightfully satisfying as a well-kept secret.

****

The dark road back to Blake's Folly was relatively empty. Soft music played on the car radio. Now what would happen? She had been pretty sure that Lance's offer to pick her up and take her to the Three Penny Inn wasn't a show of gallantry. No, once he was in her territory, standing in front of her door, he would expect to be invited in for a coffee. For a chance to be alone together.

Of course, that didn't mean he expected they would leap into bed together. No, somehow she felt that Lance's technique was far more sophisticated. Like her, he preferred the slow dance, the sweet promise of intimacy, more than its conclusion. Except that, at this moment, neither the dance nor the promise captivated her. Not tonight. The idea of an affair with Lance had lost its appeal. Perhaps not for forever, but for the moment anyway.

Lance left the main highway, turned down the narrower, icier road leading into Blake's Folly. Stopped in front of her shop. The car's motor purred.

"Thank you for the lovely evening."

He smiled. "The pleasure was mine."

"Drive safely." And in a softer voice, "Good night, Lance."

"Good night, Rose." Lance leaned in closer toward her, lifted her chin with one finger, kissed her. A nice kiss. Gentle. Seductive. Promising.

One that almost had her wanting more. Almost. But not quite.

She leaned against the door of her shop, watching as the taillights of Lance's car disappeared. Remembered standing in this same place last night with Jonah. How she would have loved to reach out, snuggle her arm through his as they'd walked through the icy night streets after leaving the Mizpah, but she couldn't. When they'd arrived here, at her door, she hadn't invited him inside, either—wouldn't that have seemed like an overt invitation to intimacy? Even so, her lips had almost ached for his. If he'd been a free man, a kiss would have been perfectly normal…and possibly quite wonderful.

Wasn't she imagining their interest was mutual? Yes, she was. It was wishful thinking only. Jonah made absolutely no move to touch her, had given no hint that he desired physical contact. He had remained affable and impersonal. Like a friend. So, they'd stood here silently for a few minutes, as if neither had wanted to end the evening. Until, finally, like good friends who sincerely enjoyed each other's company, they had merely bid each other good night.

Chapter Five: Elsa

Rose carefully picked her way over the booby-trapped terrain leading up to the battered, long-out-of-commission trailer her mother lived in. "Home sweet home," she muttered as she avoided three unsavory-smelling, exploding plastic sacks of garbage.

She hated coming here. Hated the mound of empty bottles heaped behind the trailer, right alongside an abandoned and rusted-out propane stove, a gutted RV fridge, and a moldering pile of cast-off clothing. She would have avoided this social call if she could have, but since she and her mother lived in the same community (no one could say Blake's Folly was a town these days, not with its population of fifty-three odd souls), dropping by was a necessity. Or perhaps a duty she performed out of guilt—although why she should feel guilty for someone else's failure was beyond her comprehension.

However, she also knew if she didn't come see her mother from time to time, Elsa would come staggering over the horizon, three sheets to the wind, looking for her daughter and spewing out reproach to each and every man or woman she crossed along the way. If Rose truly hoped to avoid the mother-daughter "relationship," she'd have to move so far away that Elsa would never find her. That probably meant residence in a bathysphere, deep down in the Bering Sea's

Zhemchug Canyon.

Yet, she didn't want to move away. She loved this beat-up has-been community, the smell of dusty desert air, the dry nippy winds, and the way the bleached light illuminated the bleak hills. She treasured the silence; she reveled in the loneliness. Coming back here after all the years in noisy, crowded places, did really feel like she'd come home. And this home was the right place for her too...even if her mother was always within howling distance.

Suppressing a resigned groan, Rose raised her hand and tapped on the trailer door's dull plastic.

"Yeah? Whaddya want?" The usual warm welcome.

"Elsa? It's me. Rose." She opened the door.

Inside, the air was smoke-filled, and the television blasted out a late-morning comedy show. Her mother and Alf Paltry, drinking glasses in one hand, burning cigarettes in the other, gazed over at her with bleary-eyed recognition. Rose knew it was going to be a lousy visit, as usual.

"Well, look what the cat dragged in."

"Nice to see you too, Elsa." Rose could never bring herself to call the woman "mother." To her, it would have made a mockery of that innocent two-syllable word. She turned to the man at her side.

"Hi, Alf. How are you doing?"

Alf nodded. He was, at the best of times, a man of few words; at the worst, he was the stony silent type.

Elsa launched into her next attack. "Doan see yer face much 'round here. Can't be bothered, of course."

Rose didn't waste energy answering. She looked around for an empty chair, a perch, anyplace where she could sit comfortably for a five-minute visit. There wasn't one. Clothes, papers, groceries, over-filled ashtrays topped every surface and threatened to topple floor-ward at the slightest vibration. Closing the door firmly behind her, she leaned against it. She wouldn't be staying for long, anyway.

"What have you been doing with yourself, Elsa?" She forced herself to look interested in whatever answer came, although her mother's daily activities were perfectly clear: drinking, smoking, watching television.

"You so innerested allava sudden?" Elsa's little eyes set in a puffy face were hostile. She'd been a great beauty in the days before cigarettes and booze had taken their toll. In the days when she'd thought she'd had a dream to follow. "What's it to you anyways?"

"Apparently, you corralled Ned Stalks yesterday, told him you hadn't seen me for weeks. That I had no loyalty, that I was a waste of time, that the least I could do was come around and help you, poor woman, with something that needed urgent attention."

"Goddamn truth."

"So, here I am. Tell me, what was so urgent? What did you need my help for?"

In lieu of an answer, Elsa squashed out the cigarette burning between her fingers, shook out another one from the pack nestled beside her thigh, lit it, took a deep drag, and started coughing, a phlegmy hacking sound. When she managed to catch her breath, she gasped out: "No point now. Too late. Knew I couldn't count on you."

Rose pushed down her feeling of annoyance. As ever, her mother blamed everyone else in the world for her dissatisfaction. It would have been intolerable for

Elsa to accept that she'd been entirely responsible for the direction her life had taken, for the wreck she had become. Yet, Rose remembered how much she had once admired her—despite her incompetence as a caring maternal figure. Elsa had been so beautiful in her younger days, with her sleek blond hair, lovely skin, and large expressive eyes. Her singing voice had been as sweet as a nightingale's, and she could have gone far with it. She might never have become the famous star she thought she should be, but she certainly would have been able to make a living as a singer. To have gone on the road with good musicians, to have experienced the fast-paced city life she had always dreamt about.

Elsa's love of alcohol had been her fatal flaw. Unable to make auditions, too drunk to perform, she had frightened off potential employers; other musicians had scrupulously avoided her. The few people willing to tolerate her impossible behavior, at least for a while, were the many lovers attracted by her soon-jaded beauty.

Although Rose knew she was unlike her mother, she saw their similarities. Once upon a time, she, too, had tried to carve out a career as a singer; she, too, had seen how easy it was to fall from grace. Unlike her mother, she had picked herself up and, through sheer willpower, steered her life in another direction.

What about her attitude to men? Weren't they alike in that way too? Her mother had, in earlier days, used her outstanding looks to attract attention. Rose, although less classically beautiful, knew she also charmed in the same way.

"So whaddya jus' standin' there for? Whaddya want from me?"

This stopover wasn't going to get chummier. Rose put her hand on the handle of the trailer door. "I'm driving into Reno this afternoon. I wanted to know if you need anything. Anything useful, that is. Food, clothes…"

"What's it to you?"

Rose screwed up her lips in a saccharine smile. "Great seeing you both again. I'll be back in a year or two."

"Yeah, right. Jus' run away like you always do. Too busy making money hand over fist in that junk store of yours to bother with us, of course."

"You know of a junk store in the desert that makes money hand over fist?" Rose had long experience in circumventing nosy questions and potential manipulation. Her mother would be more than happy to hear her daughter was doing well enough to fork over enough cash for the week's supply of vodka.

Elsa couldn't be bothered answering. She had lost all interest in Rose. Her eyes had gone back to the television screen, to the antics of three comedians dressed in shaggy bear costumes, to the roar of the studio audience.

If her admirers could see her now, Rose mused, then she wouldn't seem so glamorous or so desirable. Perhaps Lance would have second thoughts about inviting her to posh restaurants: he was a veterinarian, an educated man. And what about Jonah? Oh yes, she could picture his reaction. This little scene would more than convince him she was way off the map as far as a serious friendship was concerned. She almost howled out loud at the picture that came to mind: the one in which she and Jonah Livingstone, Dr. University

Professor, Dr. Geology, were strolling hand in hand to this same trailer for a friendly family visit with Alf and Elsa. What a joke.

****

That evening, Rose parked her car, turned off the headlights, and waited a few moments to make certain no one had followed her here. It was an unnecessary precaution. Who would follow her these days? No one. Her vigilance was a reflex from the time when a violently jealous and drugged husband could mean big trouble. Since this was also a delicate situation—although less of a personal one—she felt honor bound to employ the same stealth. Finally, convinced that the streets were calm, that no one was watching, she stepped out onto the sidewalk and pulled a suitcase out of the back seat.

Bright stars winked merrily as she made her way up the crazy paving to the little house in this unpretentious Reno suburb. The night was amazingly cold, the roads were still icy, and the long drive from Blake's Folly had been arduous. She was pleased the journey was over—until tomorrow morning's return trip.

Rose rang the doorbell three times in a code that told the residents she was the one at the door. She did have her own key, and she used it when she returned here late at night. If she let herself into the house while everyone was wide-awake, she would feel as though she were intruding on the privacy of the three women who lived here. That would have been offensive to her.

It was Ana who opened the door, her eyes warm and welcoming, and she hugged her with sincere affection. Then, because it was a bitter winter evening, she bundled Rose into the tiny kitchen, began preparing a big mug of her specialty: Mexican hot chocolate mixed with cinnamon and chili powder.

Rose closed her eyes, sniffed the fragrant spicy treat. She loved coming here, to this homey, crowded little house. She adored the women who lived here, the odor of the exotic foods they cooked, the excessive and colorful decor of the tiny rooms, the warm chatter. This was a whole world away from her life in Blake's Folly; it was also a world away from the life these women had once known: all three—Ana, Teresa, and Silvia—were illegal immigrants.

While she savored the steamy cup of liquid chocolate, she and Ana exchanged the week's news. Then they went into a little back room where two sewing machines and a large worktable were squeezed into a space also containing a lumpy sofa bed. Rose opened the suitcase she had brought with her, pulled out the cloth she had so carefully cut. Ana lifted one hand, caressed the soft fabric, and smiled. Rose knew that explanations were unnecessary. Ana was the most talented seamstress she had ever worked with, and Rose paid her and Teresa as much as she could manage. It was her way of acknowledging their expertise.

She knew the women's stories: Ana had survived the long walk through the desert after being abandoned by the coyote or smuggler who took those without legal papers across the border. Supplied with enough food and water for two days, she had, fortunately, survived long enough to reach help in a local community. The two people who had been with her, hadn't been so lucky. As for Teresa, she had paid two thousand dollars to a coyote who had shown her where she could crawl through a hole in the border fence. Silvia had come to the country earlier, had remained here for twenty years after her visa had run out. All three women were raising—or had raised—children who were American citizens and attended school. All three lived in the shadows, because they feared deportation and separation from those children. Still, she knew that Tereza and Ana, like many Mexicans in the country, dreamt of returning home one day when their children were independent.

"Immigrants always miss the place we were raised in. We miss our own culture."

Rose knew she could do nothing to make up for the constant anxiety the women lived with, or for tragedies in their past—domestic tragedy, brutal drug-cartel violence, the lack of schooling in rural towns—but providing employment was one way she could help. Silvia, employed elsewhere, used a Social Security number bought on the black market. Like other illegals doing the same thing, she paid taxes but was unable to get a refund. As for Ana and Teresa, their sewing skill had helped make Rose's little business a success.

Yes, what she was doing was illegal. Although the Universal Declaration of Human Rights stated that no person be denied the right to work, Rose knew the government circumvented that right by making it illegal for American citizens to hire undeclared immigrants inside the country. It was a risk she was willing to take, a risk she could live with—and with a good conscience.

The women paid property tax on this little house, a tax that paid for the public schools their children attended. Their children, determined to succeed, to become educated professionals, were excellent students. Rose was certain they would do fine. In her mind, providing Ana and Teresa with work was her way of righting a wrong: equalizing, in her own modest way, the injustice that two nations sharing the same border had one of the largest income gaps on Earth.

****

"You look beautiful." Ana nodded with approval when, an hour later, Rose emerged from the back bedroom dressed quite differently. The skirt she wore was full, red, and swinging: the beautifully embroidered sleeves of a white blouse flowed from her tight, brocaded vest. Her golden hair, braided and pinned, was partly covered by a silvery cloth headband.

"Thank you, Ana. It's your flair that created such lovely clothes."

"All I did was sew them together. The talent is yours."

Rose merely shrugged. "I copied what other women created for hundreds of years in Russia. They made their own clothes, and they did all the embroidery themselves. My grandmother tried to teach me needlework, but I was hopeless at it."

"We're all gifted in different ways."

"Maybe." She snuggled into her warm coat, kissed Ana on the cheek, then locking the front door behind her, tripped back down the walk to her car, her feet in their soft pointed shoes moving noiselessly on the flat paving stones.

Ten minutes later, she parked close to a brightly lit, unpretentious clapboard building, once an abandoned community center of sorts, now spruced up by fresh white paint and sporting a sign written in the Cyrillic alphabet. As she made her way toward the front door, her pulse quickened. The rippling of notes from the beautiful bayan filled the frosty night, and the sound touched something deep inside her soul.

For if she claimed that her mother had named her after a crystal formation found in Oklahoma, that wasn't the whole story. It had been her grandmother who had insisted the name stick, for she had been born in Bobriki, a small Russian village, where red roses and bright green leaves had once been embroidered on blouses and skirts, where those rosy garlands were the motif of headscarves and the painted decoration on house beams. Having a grandchild named Rose had been a sentimental gesture, one that conjured up lost days and a village first smothered by Soviet repression, then destroyed by war.

In this shabby building with its makeshift stage, Rose found a trace of that past. How she looked forward to these Saturday evenings! She pushed open the front door that opened directly into the main room. Up at the front, already seated on the stage, were the people she loved with all her heart: Galina, Sergei, Andrei, Borya, Bogdan, George, Ivan, and Boris. In their hands were the most beautiful instruments in the world: the triangular balalaikas in their various sizes from the highest-pitched to the lowest, the strange and wonderful pear-shaped stringed gudok, and the accordion-like bayans. Her heart sang as she joined the musicians on the dais.

Here was where she felt most alive, most comfortable. Here was the real excitement in her life. This was her home—her true home—deep in her secret world.

Chapter Six: Alice

"Right from the beginning, it was an instant attraction. Instant. Impossible." Rose looked out of the big window of her workroom, sighed dramatically.

"An instant attraction? You seem to have a lot of those." Alice Treemont's tone was mocking.

Rose turned back to her friend, threw her a sour look. "Sure, I do. So what? Instant attractions make life fun. When they're impossible, the fun is sucked out of them."

Alice guffawed and not with sympathy, either.

Of course, Alice would never understand how she functioned. Alice wasn't the sort of person who would indulge in an instant attraction. Take a look at how she was dressed: big walking boots, sagging woolen stockings, an ancient and wrecked sweater, a shapeless, colorless skirt. How did she get her hands on dreadful clothes like those? Even junk shops would refuse them. Yet, somehow, on Alice's long lanky body, everything came together in a strange glamour; and with her hair braided into two long pigtails, she was more like a 1920s movie star than a fashion reject.

"Well, perhaps another instant attraction will wander into your store today, and you'll forget all about this last one."

"You're wrong." Rose's chin tilted defiantly. But was Alice really wrong? Yes, she craved sudden attractions and the hint of passion, but that was part of a game. Somehow, she didn't feel that the instant attraction she had shared with Jonah Livingstone had been on the same, superficial level. She could see why Alice would think and say that, though.

"Fine. Men do seem to have those instant moments when they see me. I bring out their conquering caveman instinct: big blue eyes, blond curls, a waist, boobs, and hips—those will do it every time. But those instant attractions are never mutual." She paused. Raised her hands in a gesture that was definitely self-mocking. "Okay, okay. Sometimes they're mutual. The thing I felt *this* time was different. He is wonderful-looking, at least I think he is. You wouldn't. He's all uneven, craggy sharp angles."

"But you won't tell me his name."

"Because there's no point. He was someone passing through Blake's Folly, that's all." Which was a little white lie. What was the real reason? Because she didn't want to give too much importance to the time spent with Jonah in the Mizpah. Because saying his name made him more real, and that wasn't a good idea. Rose shook her head. "Why am I talking about the guy now? What am I trying to do? Talk myself into falling in love? I am an idiot!"

"You're talking about him because I—very innocently—asked you if any new customers had come in." Alice smirked. "And your answer came out with far more passion than I expected."

"Right." Rose chewed her lips. "Because talking with him was wonderful. Incredible. The subjects we touched on: prehistory—because he's a geologist—and climate change, political views, beliefs. It was fascinating to discover how much we seem to have in common…despite the differences in our education and in the lives we lead. We probably could have talked all night, except Ned Stalks broke into the conversation, yawned rudely, then announced it was midnight and he was closing up shop."

"You feel that this man—whose name you refuse to divulge—is attracted to you, too? That he'd be willing to join all the other men around you, become another devoted member of the Rose Badger Admiration Society?"

"That's the point. I don't. Not really. I get the feeling he's different from the other men I know. I could be wrong, of course."

Alice nodded. "You might be. You might never find out either."

"No. That's true enough. Because he's attached, and attached men are definitely out of the running as far as I'm concerned."

"If he weren't?"

"If he were free? I think he would be more than another one of my admirers. He's too…too interesting for that. I like him too much. Yet, even if I feel that way about him, it's one-sided. I'm sure he likes my company. He probably finds me attractive. He really does want me as a friend. He actually came out and said that."

Alice sighed. "So what's the problem? You don't like the idea of someone not falling madly in love with you? Not thinking you're the most seductive woman on earth?"

Rose shrugged. "Maybe." She stood, went over to her worktable, smoothed out the sheet of pattern paper lying there. Yes, she'd seen the way Jonah looked at her, and she was certain he'd appreciated what he'd seen. No doubt, he'd also realized how wide the gulf was between them, even if he had no details. He worked as a geologist; she ran a small boutique selling clothes and a few perfectly useless, odd relics. He lived in Reno; she lived in Blake's Folly, a quaint, bashed-up community filled with cranks, originals, her alcoholic mother, and her mother's alcoholic paramour. Highly educated, he had probably always led a steady and disciplined life. Her own past, one she kept hidden, had been rocky, destructive, ugly.

Besides, why fret? A man as wonderfully appealing as Jonah Livingstone would never stand the test of time, would he? Sure, he was different from the other men she knew; her reaction to him had certainly been immediate. In the long run, if he were free, if they could have a relationship, the dazzle would vanish quickly enough. Life together would become ho-hum. It always did, didn't it? Of course it did. The thought of ho-hum dismayed her. Why exchange the thrill of endless instant attractions for ho-hum?

"Okay, fine," she said briskly. "Now that we've covered all aspects of my hopeless, silly crush, we're going to drop the subject, okay? Let's say I had a brief, secret passion, and it was one that could never go anywhere—at least, not with him, it can't. The whole experience was no more than a tingle of imaginary warmth to heat up winter's chill."

"Fine. We'll stop this mindless girlie-talk conversation—for the time being, anyway. Now, here's another topic of some importance." Alice's pale eyes met hers. "You need a dog."

"I need a what?"

"A dog."

"A dog? You must be joking. I definitely don't need a dog. No way do I need one. What put this new and crazy idea into your head? The fact that I have a crush on an unavailable man? And you think a dog is the perfect solution?"

"No. Not because of that. Because I don't like the idea of you working in this store all alone until late in the evening."

"What's that supposed to mean?"

"It means I'm looking out for your safety. There are a lot of cranks out there in the big wide world. You need something around that's big, warm, fuzzy, and protective. Something with big teeth and a quick temper."

"Oh, right. Why don't you try and convince me to adopt a pet rattler? Isn't that more up your street as a herpetologist?"

Alice looked smug. "Rattlers don't have teeth. They aren't fuzzy, either. They have scales, as you well know."

"Look, I know what you're up to. You've probably had another stray dumped on you, and your house is filled to capacity, am I right? So you think you can convince me, like you convince everyone else, to adopt one of your mutts. Well, take a look around. There are fabrics here, dresses, hats, and delicate things. Things that would attract dog hair in no time at all. Hairy clothes are something no customer would tolerate."

"A dog would also be perfect company for you. The one I'm thinking of is called Noodle. He's part shepherd, part something curly, and part who knows what. He belonged to a family who moved to Sacramento. They dumped him, so he needs a good home." Like any obsessional person, Alice was not to be deflected when she had an idea in her head. "You have room for a dog, too. Look at all this space. Think of the fun you'll have going for walks with Noodle in the desert."

"Going for walks in the grim landscape that's all around this godforsaken town doesn't sound like my idea of fun. It sounds like the opposite of fun." Rose waved her arm, gestured toward the workshop's large, old-fashioned windows. Outside, morning light shimmered on the thin veil of snow covering the lumpy-looking frozen ground. "Out there, it's icy cold. Not in here, though. In here, it's bright, toasty, and comfortable, thanks to that large stove in the corner. Here, is where I want to be."

She loved this workspace, the crowded front room shop, and the adjoining back rooms where she lived. After the local newspaper had folded in 1908, this building had been taken over by a furniture maker in the 1920s, but that desperate attempt to eke out a living in an inhospitable environment had failed. Nowadays, only hopeless dreamers clung to life out here.

"How did your dinner with Lance Potter go?" Alice asked suddenly.

Rose almost jumped. She'd been so lost in thought, she'd forgotten her friend was still there, sitting in the big chair near the stove's heat. "Back to besotted adolescent talk, are we?" She smirked. "Okay, then. The dinner with Lance was nice."

"Nice? Only nice?"

"Yes, fine. Great food. Lovely wine."

"Great food? Lovely wine? That's it? Less than a week ago, you gave me the impression he was the man of the moment."

"Did I?"

"He's lost his place as number one candidate for a love affair?"

"I admit I didn't do much to encourage him."

Alice's brows rose—she probably doubted her every word: according to Alice, Rose never stopped sending available signals to any male in the area.

Rose groaned. "Alice, you must believe me this time. I'm pretty sure Lance is not the man for me."

"Why? What's wrong now?"

"Look, Lance is the romantic hero type of man, the one all the women have crushes on because he's gorgeous and charismatic. He's also a serial lover, never settling down, and never taking any one woman seriously for long. You can't risk becoming—even temporarily—attached to someone like that. For me, that dims some of his glitter. When the glitter goes, life becomes real again. Normal. Ordinary. Everyday existence with no sparks in it."

"Sparks," Alice muttered. "And by the way, that sounds very much like a description of you. Collecting admirers, looking gorgeous, never taking anyone seriously."

Rose's eyes narrowed. "Okay, maybe it does, and perhaps that's why Lance and I aren't meant to go further than a flirtation. We're too alike. But unlike Lance, I have a reason for being the way I am. I was married once, remember? I did actually commit, and that experience cured me of the need to do it again."

"Once bitten, twice shy?"

"Apt words from a dog-rescue fanatic." Leaning back against the worktable, Rose crossed her arms. It was time she stopped being defensive and retaliated a little. "Don't try to tell me that you don't know what sparks are. What's going on with Jace Constant?"

Alice's usually pale cheeks turned a fragile pink, but she didn't answer.

"Because every single person in Blake's Folly has noticed what happens every time Jace Constant, that new lodger of yours, comes anywhere within a three-thousand-mile radius of you. Sweetheart…you're both the talk of the town."

Alice stood abruptly and pulled on her shabby coat, one that had seen its best, most fashionable, days circa forty years ago. "See you around."

"Without a doubt," answered Rose breezily, not in the least affected by her closest friend's sudden departure. She was used to her cranky ways, knew that Alice would rather chew nuts and bolts than come out and admit she might actually *feel* something for another human being. She seemed to have as many secrets as Rose did—perhaps that was why they sought each other's company: they both knew neither would pry into forbidden territory, then smear the information around.

"By the way," she called to Alice's back before the door closed, "you can forget about the dog. No way will I accept a dog in my life."

Through the wide windows of the workroom, Alice was a mere stick figure on the broad panorama, marching out toward the edge of Blake's Folly and the world of frozen scrub and dun-colored earth. Who knew what she was up to now? Probably tracking down venomous snakes to love and coddle, or looking for abandoned dogs to nurture. Well, good luck to her.

Rose picked up her tape measure and pencil, set to work on a new "vintage" creation, one bound to dazzle the most discriminating, sharp-eyed lady so that she would forget to notice all the signs that screamed new, not antique. And because she was a lighthearted and happy person, Rose sang as she worked, her voice rising in the high tones of authentic Russian folk music, the vocal register called "white sound." The songs told of village life, fertile fields, long-lost battles, foiled love, and they'd come directly from the Russian steppe via her grandmother. They had been her inheritance, a very precious one.

****

At noon, the bell above the shop door tinkled. Rose emerged from her work area in the back, and found, instead of a potential customer, rancher Roy Palmer. Shifting from foot to foot, he threw unhappy sideways glances at the frilly blouses, the racks of dresses, and the secondhand coats. Roy felt like a bull in a china shop whenever he came here, and that amused Rose greatly; he was miserably uncomfortable with the lacy, sexy, feathers-and-glitter side of womanhood. She, with her flirtations, fluff, and falderals, probably terrified him; he would only be truly comfortable with earthy, practical females who put him at his ease and talked openly about animal husbandry. Still, he couldn't keep away. Roy was as attracted to her as a magpie is to glitter.

She couldn't say she minded. He was a calm, steady man, tall, muscular, hazel-eyed. You could sense his strength and stability as soon as he walked into a room. Yes, a man like that was highly prized. Could she encourage him? She couldn't, although she knew it would take one come-hither glance on her part for him to become her lifelong devoted paramour.

Taking his hand, she led him to one of the deep, plush armchairs reserved for visitors.

"Coffee?"

"Uh, well…no."

Rose almost burst out laughing. News about her incompetence in cooking had spread far and wide. She sat down in the armchair opposite Roy.

"What are you doing here in town today?"

"I was passing through. I was out at the Jenkinses' ranch for a look-see. Ted was doing a breeding-soundness examination." With that, he launched into his favorite topic: cattle breeding with its inspection of genital organs, assessment of sperm production and quality, semen collection via electro-ejaculation.

Rose listened as she always did—being a good listener was one of her exceptional abilities—and wondered if this line of conversation could ever fit into any woman's daily life. Roy was definitely on the lookout for a wife to keep him company out on that lonely ranch of his. There were a few single women in the area, and some of them were desperate to find a mate, but they must find Roy rough going. She feared he was slated to remain alone unless, by some rare chance, a fairy godmother from the rancher's union intervened and hooked him up with a female who adored incredibly long conversations about gestation periods, birthing techniques, and animal libido.

"How about dinner on Saturday evening?" Roy was saying.

Rose snapped back into the present. She had forgotten she was sitting here in her shop, listening to Roy's monologue. How rude. Had he noticed? Probably not. She shook her head. "Sorry, Roy. Saturday's out. I have to be in Reno."

Roy's brow furrowed. "You're often in Reno on Saturdays."

"That's where I pick up the best merchandise. The weekend is when most people are free and can show me things they want to get rid of." The excuse didn't sound totally convincing to her ears, but she didn't really care. What did Roy—or anyone else—know about the secondhand rag trade? Not enough to question her. She wouldn't tell anyone what she really did in Reno.

"Okay. How about lunch today?"

"Now?"

"You have to eat. It's lunchtime. You hate cooking."

"I don't hate cooking," said Rose with a happy smile. "I couldn't possibly hate it, because I avoid it like the plague. Everyone knows that too." Especially the male admirers who preferred being seen with her, wining and dining her.

Roy sniggered. "Then it's lunch at the Mizpah."

****

When Rose and Roy entered the ever brightly lit Mizpah Saloon, everyone turned—almost in unison—to rubberneck. Of course, they did. All present were the same barflies that were here every other day, and they were still jawing on about the world going to hell. Her arrival, with yet another man in tow, was sure to get their tongues waggling at turbo speed.

Not ten minutes later, the interest level stepped up

a few notches with the sudden appearance of Mike Dowd, firefighter. Impervious—or completely indifferent—to the fact that he was elbowing in on Roy's invitation, he slid into the booth, made himself at home, looked at her lovingly. Thankfully, he steered the conversation away from bovine reproduction and onto fire-safe landscaping. Rose didn't actually find it a passionately interesting subject, but the barflies moved in closer, in case the topic became bawdy. Wasn't that what they expected when she was around?

Well, so what? She could live with their silly ideas and suspicions, for everyone here in the Mizpah had almost as much information about local history as she did. All knew that, a few streets away, quite a few of those shabby, disused buildings along Main Street had once housed the lowest saloons and brothels. That, in some, the "ladies" would sit in the wide windows, illuminated by red lights, with their lap dogs on their knees. Loved by the miners, cowboys, and ranchers, they had also been welcomed by local shopkeepers, for they spent their hard-earned cash on fans, furs, clothes, all manner of fluffy and shining gewgaws. It had been the local wives who had detested the ladies of pleasure, and their disapproval had condemned them to the last row at social events and theatrical performances in the local community hall and during church services.

Although their silks, gaudy jewels, and perfumes set them apart from "decent" town women, the madams made certain their "girls" were well-behaved and lady-like in public. In reality, they had no reason to be otherwise: although a few were tough, gritty women, most were those who, through bad luck, circumstance, or personal choice, had come to work in the sex trade.

They were as sentimental and vital as any other woman, crying each Christmas over the memory of faraway homes, inaccessible families, and a way of life no longer open to them. Rose knew that, because her warm-hearted and generous paternal grandmother had been one of those "fallen women." And her paternal grandfather had been one of her clients.

But all that was in the past. Local houses of ill fame had closed after the town's complete decline, although they remained legal elsewhere in Nevada. To Rose, prostitutes were social workers of a sort. Who were those who condemned them? Some of those disapproving folk were standing up at the bar right now. Yet, not a few of them were, like her, the direct descendants of those long-gone, good-time girls: talk about people in glass houses!

Did Roy notice the disapproving glances? Probably not. What about Jonah? What would he have said if he knew her family history? As a university professor, he had a good reputation to keep up. Of course, he did. He wouldn't risk it for a Rose Badger. Unless she was getting it all wrong, letting herself be influenced by her own fear of inferiority. If so, that was stupid. She had to stop condemning herself. Jonah was intelligent and open-minded. What if he thought her past was colorful? Amusing. Titillating.

Come on, Rose Badger. Cut this out immediately. How did she know she'd see Jonah again? She might not. Unless someone in the scientific world suddenly discovered that Blake's Folly was the ichthyosaur capital of the world a few hundred million years ago.

Chapter Seven: Fossils

She was dead wrong. Jonah phoned her on Tuesday afternoon, and it didn't take a nanosecond to recognize his deep rich voice.

"Rose?"

"Jonah."

He whistled. "That was fast."

"I've got a good ear." She felt like kicking herself. Now he'd think she'd been hanging over her telephone, hoping he'd call. She *had* been hoping he'd call, of course, but she definitely hadn't been hanging over the telephone—her life was too interesting for wasting time like that.

"Are you still serious about wanting to see fossils?"

"Of course I am. I don't change my mind that easily."

"How about tomorrow morning, then? I could pick you up at nine. Unless, of course, you have to be in your shop…" His voice trailed off.

He sounded as though he might be disappointed if she refused. "Nine o'clock is fine. I'll ask Lucy Barnes to keep the shop open for me. Whenever I ask her to come in and take charge of Second Hand Rose, she's thrilled. She's a lousy saleswoman, but being here gives her a warm place to sit and wait for Salticidae."

"For what?"

"Jumping spiders."

"Jumping spiders?"

"Lucy claims they're the most beautiful spiders in the state of Nevada. But let's not go there. She's another crank."

"Right. Back to fossils. Do you have good shoes for walking? I have to go out to the old Winterback Mine, and the terrain is pretty rough—more so with all the ice and hard-packed snow."

"Of course, I have good walking boots. That's what being a country girl is all about." She smiled to herself. The inhospitable beige terrain in this area resembled a moonscape more than any normal person's idea of countryside.

"It will be cold too."

"No kidding. You think it's toasty in Blake's Folly today?"

When she hung up the phone, she felt like dancing, jumping in the air, clapping her hands. *Ridiculous.* The word pounded through her head with all the force of a jackhammer. Was she nuts? The lifestyle Jonah led with Marina was probably as foreign to her own as a yurt colony in backwoods Mongolia was to a brownstone mansion in New York's city center.

Yet, despite all the warnings she gave her heart and all the negative arguments, she couldn't damp down her excitement. She'd be seeing Jonah the next morning. Incredible. Then she ordered herself to calm down. She'd never have more than friendship with Jonah? Well, so what? Friendship with Jonah Livingstone sounded like a great idea.

****

They sat on a low wall on the frozen hillside above

the mine. Jonah cupped the perfectly preserved ammonite fossil in the palm of his hand.

"It's so tiny," said Rose. "A flat little snail."

"This one is. But the largest known ammonites are over six feet in diameter, and they had a lot more in common with modern octopuses, squid, and cuttlefish than snails. They were free-swimming, so you find ammonite fossils almost everywhere in the world. Medieval Europeans thought they were petrified coiled snakes, so they called them serpent stones. Many believed they had healing or oracular powers. Native Americans couldn't understand their significance either, so they invented wonderful myths to explain their presence."

She looked at him shyly. "Do you have Native American blood? You look a bit like a Shoshone."

She was astute, he noted. "Perhaps I have a few Shoshone genes. On my paternal grandfather's side, we're Northern Paiute, not Shoshone, but the Western Shoshone and Northern Paiute are culturally close to each other. We've also been intermingling with the Washoe people, once our traditional enemies, on reservations in the Reno area for at least a hundred years, so I'll never know for certain. Not that it matters. My grandfather married my grandmother, a half-Southern Paiute schoolteacher from Idaho, and her father originally came from Sweden. My mother's parents are Italian, so the mix is quite complete."

"How wonderful. It's a bit like my own heritage," said Rose. "Mine sounds less exotic, though."

"How so?"

"I'm Russian on my maternal grandmother's side."

"Russian?"

"Yes." She nodded. "What most people don't know is that Russian-Americans are the largest ethnic group in the United States after Mexican-Americans. Most were born in the former Soviet Union. My grandmother Polina snuck out of the country as the war was ending. She knew nothing about America, but she came out west, to Nevada, to look for work in the casinos."

Jonah was impressed. "She must have been a courageous lady."

"She was, you know. She spoke only rudimentary English, and I don't know how she survived. Then she met my grandfather, Cal, and he fell in love with her as soon as he caught sight of her. He dragged her back here, to Blake's Folly boredom, and life as a star singer in a failing saloon, the Red Nag."

"Did she love him?"

"Oh, yes. She did. Deeply. When Cal died, she was inconsolable."

"And on the paternal side?"

Her lips were twitching. "My paternal grandmother was a local lady who mated with a passing stranger, variety unknown. Then she married someone else."

"Interesting."

"Interesting?"

There had been the hint of challenge in her voice, and she was watching him closely. Had she expected him to be shocked by the disclosure of her father's unknown parentage? Were such things important?

"Yes, interesting, because it leaves the door open to much exotic speculation."

"You think so?" She didn't look so certain about that.

"And the Russian side explains your naturally

73

blond hair and pale blue eyes. It's a nice heritage indeed." So was the wide Slavic bone structure of her face. Combined with the finely drawn mouth and softly arching brows, the result was enchanting—as enchanting as her curiosity about his work, her bubbling playfulness, and the feisty resilience he sensed in her.

A blast of icy desert wind buffeted them. She didn't so much as shiver, Jonah noticed. True, she was well bundled under her woolly hat, thick scarf, and winter coat, but most of the women he knew would be complaining bitterly.

"What are all those men doing way down there, wandering around?" Rose asked.

"They're scientists and members of the preservation society. They're assessing the site's potential as a nature reserve. There has been a certain amount of political pressure to open the area as a tourist attraction, but old mining areas always pose problems. Improperly treated mining waste creates toxic dust. Poisons like arsenic, boron, mercury, and uranium have filtered into the ground, polluted drinking water."

As always, she listened soberly, taking in everything he said. He was surprised by her concentration: normally, people yawned with boredom when he launched in on his favorite topics. "Of course, cleanup operations do prevent further damage, but it's a time-consuming process."

He stopped abruptly. Got to his feet. He was acting like a complete bore, exactly like all the pompous, educated jerks he hated. Why did every word he spoke make him sound like he was in a classroom lecturing to his students? More than anything else, he wanted to get to know Rose, discover who she was.

"How about lunch and a little warmth? Unless, of course, you have to get back to your shop…" He held his breath, hoping for more time with her.

She also rose, smiled at him. "Lunch and warmth both sound heavenly. And I understand why your work fascinates you. I love this countryside, as bleak and empty as it is, but I can't read it the way you do. I don't have the education to do that. This harshness has a special beauty, I think."

He smiled back, slowly let out his breath with relief. "It certainly does. I also love the expanse, the bleakness, like you do."

As his gaze met her limpid blue one, something—a secret meeting or a joining of souls—passed between them. Shaken, he fought the urge to reach out for her. Knew it was out of the question. At the moment.

****

The closest place was the roadside restaurant, the Dew Drop Inn. Obviously, the locale was, from the exaggerated Wild West decor, a tourist hangout in the summer months. They sat beside a large picture window in the warm room, hunched over deep bowls of hot soup.

"I really enjoyed going out to the Winterback Mine," said Rose. "Thank you for inviting me to come along." She sounded sincere.

"My pleasure." He knew he meant that too.

"I didn't really think you'd keep your promise to show me fossils and—" She stopped and caught her bottom lip in her pearly teeth, as if she had said too much, had confessed something she'd rather have kept hidden. He didn't want there to be secrets between them. He liked her too much already, and he wished he could tell her that. Knew he couldn't.

How well did he know her? Not at all. How much did they really have in common? He'd offered her friendship the other night, yet knew perfectly well his attraction was also sexual. He was willing to admit she fascinated him; a little inner voice warned him that, if he let himself go, the feeling might run deeper than that. Was that what he wanted? Why had he been so determined to see her again so quickly? Why had he invented the story about needing to be out at the mine this morning?

"And?"

She watched him from under her lashes. "And…well, I guess I didn't think you'd remember you'd made the promise."

He snickered. "I admit we geologists have the reputation of being absent-minded. We deal with time sequences of a hundred million years or so, so we have some difficulty with small-time quanta such as centuries and decades. Some of us refer to ancient civilizations as 'all that recent crap on the top.' As for deadlines, we're absolute duds." He put down his spoon, leaned back in his chair, smiled at Rose. "But I never forget a promise."

"Good to know." She leaned forward slightly. "Tell me, since you love the desert bleakness so much, what sort of place do you live in? A house with a huge garden? Or a place on a hill, overlooking the city?"

"Neither one. I live in a high-rise apartment. And yes, it does overlook the city." He stopped. It was a place that was convenient, too. Wasn't that why he'd chosen it? Convenient and impersonal. A series of rooms, not a place to get attached to.

"Oh. That's not what I imagined…" Again, she paused, and her cheeks flushed a delicate pink.

So. She'd been thinking about him too, had she? Imagining what his life was like in the same way he'd been thinking about her since they'd first met. There was a big difference, though: he was the one who did most of the talking when they were together. She was the one who asked all the questions, the one who knew how to keep the conversational ball rolling without giving out much information about herself.

He took in the flat planes of those wonderful cheekbones, the radiance in her eyes, and his heart warmed. Incredible, how much she affected him. How right it felt to be sitting across the table from her. It was almost uncanny. He needed to know more. As gently as possible, he said, "Okay, it's your turn now."

Rose stared back at him, uncomprehending. "What's my turn?"

"It hasn't escaped my notice that you have a real knack for asking questions, drawing people out. It's flattering, it won me over, and I'm certainly not the only person you've captivated, either. Being a perfect listener can also be a tactic."

She was wary, suddenly. "A tactic? What is that supposed to mean?"

"It means, it's a good way to avoid talking about yourself."

"Ah. I see." Rose looked down.

"I'm right though, aren't I?"

"There's nothing much to say. Nothing interesting, anyway." She was still refusing to look at him.

"How about if you let me be the judge of that?"

She didn't look up. Instead, began folding her table napkin into a tiny square.

"Is there a deep, dark secret you want to hide?"

Her eyes flicked up. Finally. Met his. They gave nothing away. "Okay. Fine. What is it you want to know?"

"Everything, of course." He smiled at her. "How about starting with essentials?"

She shrugged. "What sort of essentials?"

"You're hedging."

She looked away again, nodded. Looked back. Then grinned. "Okay. Guilty as charged. Not because I'm hiding any dark, treacherous secret." She dropped the folded napkin, put her elbows on the table, and crossed her arms. "Okay. Here we go. Music is important to me."

He gawked at her, nonplussed. What was secret about that? Didn't almost everyone in the world like music of one sort or another? "What kind of music?" He was prepared to be disappointed. What chance was there that their tastes coincided? No chance at all.

"My all-time favorite…" She hesitated before continuing. "Well…at the moment, anyway…my favorite is traditional Russian music."

"Russian music? Russian composers?"

She nodded, seemed unsure, remained silent.

"Russian. As in Shostakovich?"

"Shostakovich?" She blinked.

"Do you know the music of Shostakovich?" He shook his head, not because of her, but because of his own gaucherie. Why had he come up with the name of that composer? What could she possibly know of the grotesqueries, the operas, of the trials suffered by a creative genius caught in a repressive communist regime? Again, he felt like a horrific snob. Or like a man who wanted to protect himself against his own emotions, to prove that he and the lovely woman sitting across from him had little in common. "Shostakovich was a contemporary Russian composer."

Her expression changed. Vague uncertainty turned into outright annoyance. "Of course I know who Shostakovich was."

"You do?" He gaped.

"Of course," she snapped. "Why do you sound so surprised?"

"It's just that…" He stopped himself before he said something that made him look like more of a jerk. A snob. Sound more condescending.

"Go on. It's just what?"

"Not many people do know about Shostakovich," he answered quietly.

"Because I live in Blake's Folly, I wouldn't ever have heard of him? Because you don't think anyone who lives in a dying backwoods community could possibly know anything about classical music?"

Yes, of course. She'd hit the nail on the head, all right. That was exactly the reason. He could think of a few others, too. For example, how many of his friends knew anything about Shostakovich? Only the musicians and the real music lovers did. If he'd mentioned the name Shostakovich to Marina, she'd have thought he was sneezing.

She uncrossed her arms, placed her palms flat on the tabletop, leaned forward. "Do you know his arrangements of popular Russian songs?"

"Yes, I do," he said, feeling fully chastised.

"So do I. One of the reasons I know about Shostakovich is because, as I said a few brief seconds ago, I love traditional Russian music. By that, I mean traditional Russian song as well as traditional Russian instrumental music. That doesn't exclude classical music."

He sat back, staring at her, lost for words.

"Now what's the matter?" Her voice challenged. "You look as though you don't believe me."

"Oh, I believe you all right. I don't know many people who share my enthusiasm for classical music."

"I can second that, all right." To his great relief, she let out her breath, relaxed, smiled at him again. "I can't blame you for not seeing Blake's Folly as the cultural center of the world, but I grew up with classical music. My grandmother probably knew every opera ever created. Her father—my great-grandfather—was a Russian violinist. Nothing big time and famous, of course. A musician who played in provincial towns. But still…"

He pushed aside his astonishment, smiled back. "I'm also a musician. Not a professional. An amateur. But I play with a small baroque chamber group, and we use period instruments."

Her face paled, her expression was unreadable. "You're a musician?"

"Yes."

"What instrument?"

"Baroque cello."

"Incredible."

What was so incredible? He wondered at her evident surprise but kept his tone light. "Of course, most of the music we play was composed in the late seventeenth century or the early eighteenth, so Shostakovich is way too modern."

She nodded. "I should say so."

"Do you know anything about period instruments?"

"Baroque period instruments? Absolutely nothing. I could tell you about traditional Russian instruments though…" She stopped, biting her lip, as if, once again, she'd said too much.

"Traditional Russian instruments? Okay. Tell me about them."

Her hand waved in dismissal. "Another time."

"I'll hold you to that." He meant it.

"How about baroque instruments? How are they different from modern ones?"

He almost laughed out loud. Once again, she had turned the conversation around, avoided talking about herself and what she knew. He'd let her get away with it…for the moment…

"I'll tell you what. Next Friday evening, our group is giving a concert in Reno." He hesitated, held his breath. Would she be interested? Why was this so important to him? "You do get to Reno from time to time, don't you?"

"Yes, I do."

"Would you like to come hear us? I'm not saying we're so brilliant, or that the music we play is to everyone's taste, but…"

Her grin, open, wonderful, and sincere, stopped his doubts. Warmed him through and through.

"Yes, I'd love to come to your concert. Very much. Thank you for asking me."

Chapter Eight: Music

By the time Rose entered the decidedly small assembly hall, most of the seats were taken. The choice of a reduced space for the concert was deliberate, Jonah had explained. Softer, more delicate-sounding baroque instruments had been played in the intimacy of manors, palaces, and homes. "In the sixteenth and seventeenth centuries, it wasn't unusual for servants to be hired for their ability to sing or play music. It wasn't until the late 1800s that large concert halls were built for the more sonorous modern instruments and full orchestras."

She shrugged off her coat, sat, and began reading the program. Here were the names of unfamiliar instruments: the wooden traverso, recorders, a baroque oboe, baroque cellos and baroque violins, a viol da gambe, a theorbo, and a harpsichord. Amused, she noted that the composers were equally unfamiliar to her: Sermisy, Janequin, White, Gombert, Loth.

The people in the audience were also different to those she normally saw on Reno's streets. They were well dressed, calm. There was no flash; there were no loud voices. Probably, many of them were associated with the university—in other words, the sort of people Jonah normally socialized with. Definitely not the barflies at the Mizpah Saloon. How far from her world his was.

Idly, she tried to pick out Jonah's "roommate" and

remembered the designer labels Marina insisted on: she would be an elegant, assured, stylish woman. Beautiful too? Well...if she were, what did that matter? Their couple had nothing to do with her. Those thoughts, not overwhelmingly pleasant, were interrupted by the appearance of the musicians on the low stage.

She'd been with Jonah a few days ago, but seeing him again tonight was a punch in the gut. Didn't he look delicious! He'd traded in the usual leather jacket, the worn jeans, and the boots for more elegant clothes. A loose white shirt emphasized his burnished skin and Paiute beauty, while dark trousers outlined his slender hips and hugged his long legs. He was the way she'd always imagined an intellectual *should* be: cool, intelligent, strong, and sexy. Yes, she'd been right in classifying him as the fantasy man. He was never meant to play another role in her life. He was the romantic dream character, not the reality, not the person you wake up with every morning. And wasn't a perfect fantasy man more desirable than a normal human being with flaws?

The musicians tuned their instruments. There was a brief silence. Then the music began. Gentle, vibrant sounds, with an unfamiliar dissonance that bore little resemblance to the modern classical music she knew. Was it more raw sounding or more refined? Her trained musical ear picked out themes and recognized improvised ornamentation as Jonah's long fingers moved deftly over the cello's strings. The subtle lighting caressed the strong, sharp planes of his face, underlined his intensity, and his evident passion touched her profoundly. She now knew that his love of music was as deep as her own.

It was over too soon. The musicians bowed, smiled at the audience. Looking in her direction, Jonah's smile broadened. Yes, he had known she was out here, in the audience. There was an encore, of course—the audience was highly enthusiastic—then the musicians left the stage. Rose remained seated, still basking in the feelings the music had invoked, yet not certain what to do. Should she leave? She wanted to thank Jonah for the invitation, tell him how much she had enjoyed the concert, how deeply the music had moved her. What if her presence complicated things for him? How would he present her to Marina?

Instantly, she felt like kicking herself. What had she been imagining? That she was a hidden mistress? A love interest? She wasn't. Why would Marina think she was? Her relationship with Jonah was perfectly platonic, perfectly innocent. She was no rival. She was Jonah's friend. A new friend. But a friend, nonetheless.

A cluster of people waited at the front, near the dais. The musicians appeared once again, their instruments safely stowed in sacks and cases, and Jonah stopped to talk with a small group of people. No, she wouldn't wait. She would thank him the next time they spoke…whenever that might be.

She stood, slipped her arms into her woolly coat. Then, as if suddenly aware of her imminent departure—how? Telepathy? Sympathetic intelligence of some sort?—he looked over, again caught her eye. For what seemed like an eternity, their gaze held over the space separating them. In that instant, she discovered the truth: the gut-deep intensity was mutual. Her pulse accelerated; her heart beat a primitive jungle thump.

Then, as quickly as it had come, his expression

changed, became more impersonal. However intense the feeling between them might be, he wouldn't let it flower. Detaching himself from the group, he came to where she was standing.

"Did you enjoy the concert?" His eyes were merely friendly now, also questioning. Hopeful.

Did her opinion really matter to him? Maybe it did. "It was absolutely wonderful," she said with utter sincerity. "Thank you so much for introducing me to this sort of music. Thank you so much for the invitation. Thank you for making my life a bit richer."

His face softened. With pleasure—and perhaps merriment, too. Had she been gushing? Of course she had. She felt embarrassed. She should have shown as much restraint as all the other people around her. Why did she have to sound like some naïve hayseed from the sticks? Well, for heaven's sake, because she *had* breezed in from the sticks, that was why. Because she was a Blake's Folly refugee for the evening.

"You mentioned you have a place to sleep in Reno tonight?"

"I do," she confirmed. "I always stay with friends when I'm in the city."

What would he have proposed if she'd had nowhere to go? A bed in the spare room in the apartment he shared with Marina? That was a situation she was determined to avoid at all costs. Wouldn't seeing Jonah in a domestic situation rub away the magic? Make him seem more normal, more banal. She wanted to preserve the never-never fantasy for as long as she could.

"Do you have time for a late supper or at least a drink?"

85

"Of course I do." She felt blissfully happy, suddenly. Then she damped down the feeling and quickly scrutinized the auditorium. People were still chatting; others were putting on their coats and leaving, but no woman was standing patiently, looking at Jonah, and waiting for this conversation to end. "What about your…what about Marina? Isn't she here?"

His voice was dry. "Marina doesn't like classical music. She doesn't come to concerts."

"Oh."

He stood there silently for a minute, his gaze distant, as if he were caught in some internal debate. Then he sighed, met her eyes. "I think it's time we talked."

Her heart sank. She felt like clapping her hands over her ears or running away. What sort of talk would they have? She didn't want to hear about his domestic problems, didn't want to hear that he was living with a woman who didn't understand him, didn't satisfy his needs. Those were the sort of things unavailable men, married or not, poured out to the women they hoped to seduce: irritating, unacceptable conversations, meant to win a woman's pity, make her believe she alone could soothe his wounded soul. Such a conversation would destroy Jonah's appeal; it would end their friendship.

She kept her voice cool. "I'm not convinced this will be a conversation I can appreciate."

He quirked a curious eyebrow. "Meaning?"

"Domestic woes? The 'my wife—or fiancée—doesn't love me' sort of conversation?"

Any softness left his eyes. His brows became grim, unrelenting lines. "You've misinterpreted the entire situation," he said, his voice hard. "It's not your fault.

I'm the one to blame, I see that now. I didn't make things clear in the beginning. I was too busy protecting myself."

He slung the strap of his cello case over one shoulder and, taking her elbow firmly in one hand, steered her toward the exit. Then stopped, stared down at her. "Still, it would have been nice if you'd given me the benefit of the doubt. That you hadn't classified me as a man with no scruples, or shoved me into the cheating-husband category."

Which, of course, she had done, no denying: guilty as charged. If she had been entirely wrong, was it her fault? She tilted her chin defiantly.

"Weren't you the one who accused me of hiding things in my own life? I think I can say the same to you. Apparently, you also seem to keep quite a few secrets."

****

Lucky's, a small bar and restaurant, was a few blocks away, but they drove there in Jonah's car and found a parking space near the restaurant. Carefully, he lifted his cello out of the back seat and slung the strap over his shoulder again.

"You're taking that inside with you?" Rose asked. "It seems like such a bulky thing to manage in a restaurant."

"I'd never leave an instrument in a car. No musician would." Reno, although set in a pleasant landscape, was still a depressed city with a soaring crime rate. Although some claimed the situation was improving, unemployment was high. In some places, recently built housing developments were little more than ghost towns.

"I wouldn't think there are that many cello thieves

on the loose."

She was making an effort to sound lighthearted, restore the usual easy-going feeling between them, but he was angry. Not with her, of course. With himself. With his own cowardice. Her words had wounded him. So that was how she saw him: as a cheating spouse with a volley of ignoble arguments at the ready.

He shifted the cello strap into a more comfortable position. Forced himself to sound calm, normal. "Any thief seeing a large sack in a car would be tempted to take it. After discovering it was a cello, no one would know what it was worth. I can't begin to tell you how many stolen musical instruments are found in ditches or are smashed to bits and abandoned in the desert."

"Yes, of course. You're right. I've been told that the crime rate in Reno is decreasing, but I know there's still a huge problem with gangs and the drug trade."

"Don't forget the well-heeled tourists who pour in from San Francisco. They're like red flags in the eyes of local losers who believe they're the ones who should be living in life's fast lane." He managed a slight shrug. "Anyway, everyone at Lucky's is used to musicians. We often come here after rehearsals, take out our instruments, and give impromptu concerts."

"Sounds like fun."

"It is."

Once inside the restaurant, he chose a table in a quiet corner. "Are you hungry?"

Mutely, she shook her head.

His own hunger had also abated, although, after a concert, he was usually starved. Still, he ordered a selection of the savory tapas the chef was known for, and then waited until the waiter had placed two glasses of Chardonnay in front of them. How to begin this conversation? The subject was a highly uncomfortable one, and he'd been hiding his feelings for so long. Now, he knew he had to be honest—he owed that to this woman sitting in front of him. Why? Because she mattered to him. He wanted her respect, although he knew he risked losing it by telling her the truth. Wouldn't he also lose it if he lied?

"Marina and I are not a couple," he began, but to his own ears, that sounded slightly off-key. He took a deep breath, then let it out slowly. "Actually, Marina is my ex-wife."

"Oh." Rose watched him, her eyes wide. Shocked? Perhaps not. There were many emotions playing across her face, conflicting, perfectly unreadable ones. "Do you have children?"

"No, no children, thank goodness for that. Marina and I have known each other for a long time now. We started living together when we were still students, and getting married seemed like the normal thing to do. But it wasn't. What had been a college romance should have stayed that way. By the time we were both working on our doctorates, our differences were pretty obvious. I think we both knew the marriage couldn't last; we carried on out of habit. Yes, I admit it was a cowardly way to live. I kept thinking that I'd find the right moment to walk out the door. Of course, that moment never came. Marina was...is...unstable. Depressive. Overly sensitive."

In the background, soft music was playing, nothing aggressive, nothing romantic, nothing identifiable either. He sipped his wine. It was cool, pungent. "Then, one day, Marina met Matt Wilton, a big wheeler-dealer.

She announced she had fallen in love and was divorcing me." He still remembered the afternoon Marina had walked into his office at the university to tell him that. Had she expected fury? Protests of love? Never, could he have imagined the relief he'd felt.

Rose's voice was soft. "Did you mind?"

"Mind?" His mouth twisted. "Frankly, Matt was a godsend. I was finally free. A bachelor. I could follow my passion; play music whenever I chose to do so. Go to rehearsals without anyone protesting. Work out in the field for days on end and never worry about coming home for dinner. Best of all, I no longer had to feel responsible for someone with whom I had little in common."

Marina had always resented his interests. Even their taste in music clashed: he needed the complications of baroque ornamentation; she was attracted by what he considered popular commotion. A party animal, Marina needed to be surrounded by noisy friends; he was a solitary man, a lone tracker, and he never felt so complete as when out in the silence of his beloved wilderness.

"I moved into the apartment I'm living in now, and I took to single life like a duck to water. Marina and I remained friends. The peace lasted for a few blissful years, too. I was happy for her, for her successful new relationship—although I can't say I liked Matt much. He seemed a superficial sort of guy, all flash, noise, and empty brag. That was what Marina said she needed, so what difference did it make to me?"

Sitting across the table from Rose, he delighted in her lovely, seductive mouth, the beautiful eyes, but her expression was indecipherable. As usual, she was taking in his every word. Ever the good listener—that was quite an art. You could win over most of the world's population by being a good listener.

Who was Rose Badger? What did he know about her? What made her tick? Where did she stay when she was in Reno? Had she ever been married? She'd mentioned that she'd left Blake's Folly when she was younger: where had she gone? How did she survive on the meager takings of a secondhand clothes shop in Podunk, Nevada? There was so much he wanted to know, so many questions he had to ask.

For the moment, for this evening, he was the one who needed to explain, to get everything out in the open. Next time—if she were willing to see him again—he'd be the one to ask questions. He'd be the good listener; he'd insist on that.

"Why are you and Marina living together now?" Her question had no aggression in it, but it snapped him back to the present, to the hardest part of the story.

"Marina's relationship with Matt came to an abrupt and nasty end. She called me in the middle of the night: he had packed his bags and left. Over the next few weeks, we discovered that he'd cleaned out their joint account, sold off all her investments, even their house. All she had were debts. Not only that, Matt had debts all across the country. He was a petty con man, and this wasn't the first time he'd tricked a woman into trusting him."

"So you stood by her?"

"Marina tried to kill herself—twice—botched attempts, obviously. Then she went into a complete depression. She stopped functioning. She'd been a law professor, but now she couldn't work, couldn't face going outside. Since she now had nowhere to live, either, I let her move in with me. My apartment was certainly large enough for two people to live in comfortably and separately."

What else could he have done? He'd known that Marina was perfectly capable of harming herself again. In his mind, the arrangement had always been a temporary one. Not in Marina's. She didn't want to live alone. She wanted him back again—not because she loved him, he was sure of that—because she wanted to think she did.

"You still feel responsible for her?"

"I do." The problem was so difficult to explain. He wasn't sure he had correctly analyzed his own motives. Were they based on guilt because he'd been so happy without Marina, or because of something deeper, something cultural?

He sighed. "It's difficult for me to talk about this. All I can say is, this state of affairs is definitely not a permanent one. Marina has to start functioning again, taking responsibility for herself. I want my life back." How easy it was to say those words. Putting them into action, finding a solution, was another game altogether.

"Do you care about Marina very much?"

He leaned back in his seat, took a deep breath. That was another question he had avoided asking himself for quite some time. Why? Because he knew he wouldn't like the answer.

"I wonder," he said slowly. "Yes, I know how brutal that sounds. I don't love her, if that's what you're asking. Not as a husband, not as a lover, not as someone I want to live with. I know Marina is basically a good person, but I have to keep reminding myself of that.

Emotional blackmail takes its toll. It kills sympathy; it destroys empathy; and it fosters a hell of a lot of resentment."

He expected Rose to condemn him for his honesty, for letting himself be trapped and not having the strength to get out. But there was still no criticism in her gaze. She watched him with the same clear interest she always showed. So, he continued.

"Why am I in this situation? I think it's partly due to my family history. I spent a considerable amount of time with my Paiute grandfather and half-Paiute grandmother when I was growing up, and consequently, they influenced the way I am. The Paiute people have a long and tragic history. The loss of our land, our water rights, the lack of educational opportunities, all those things resulted in much poverty, many dysfunctional families, and a lot of substance abuse. One way we have of surmounting those problems is by maintaining extended families, providing solidarity and a sense of belonging. That ethic is part of me. Marina is alone in the world. She has no family, and she needs help. The least I can do is provide a solid base from which she can start again."

He stopped, briefly rubbed his eyes with his fingers, as if trying to see more clearly through the emotional fog. Then leaned forward, wanting to explain what he barely understood. "For Native Americans, patience has always been a survival tactic. And our patience is based on the belief that all things unfold in time."

Chapter Nine: Noodle

Pale wintery sun highlighted the velvety swatch of cloth spread across the worktable. Smiling with satisfaction, Rose pictured the exquisite dropped waist cocktail dress she would create—if only people would leave her in peace for a few hours. Outside the large workshop window, Alice Treemont, large plastic sack in one hand, was striding energetically over the frozen road and heading for Second Hand Rose. As usual, she was a total fashion disaster: hair in braids, a hideous print skirt, several thick and raggedy sweaters, thick woolen stockings, and clomping walking boots. And, despite all of that, she was absolutely gorgeous.

Then Rose noticed the strange-looking animal trotting along, right alongside Alice. Two minutes later, both Alice and the four-footed creature were here, standing in her workshop.

"This lovely guy is called Noodle," said Alice, pointing to the beast.

Rose grimaced. Lovely? *Come on.* "Pleased to meet you, Noodle, but if Alice thinks you're coming to stay, this will be a short friendship. There's no place for a hairy shedding animal in my store, my house, or in my life."

"Well, you'll have to change your mind. Noodle needs a good home, and you need a dog. This is an isolated building in a place that's almost a ghost town.

You need fang support."

"Fang support? What the hell is fang support? You're inventing this. I told you, I don't want a…a…" Rose looked sourly at the animal waiting calmly by Alice's feet. Okay, it had to be a dog, but she wasn't sure. "I don't want one of those. I don't want a pet of any sort."

The pet in question was the size of a large shepherd, and it had rough, unappealing fur of a splotchy beige-ish color. It also had the whiskers of a terrier, pointed ears, a corkscrew tail, and huge hairy paws. It was horribly ugly.

"Anyway, if that *is* a dog, it doesn't look anything like a dog. Okay, okay. I'm exaggerating. It *does* look like a dog—sort of. A hideous dog. Ergo, it must be a dog."

The dog gazed back at her with beautiful golden eyes. Calm eyes. Patient eyes. As if it—or he, because Alice claimed it was a male—were simply waiting for her to stop criticizing and accept him for what he was.

"What am I supposed to do with a dog?"

Alice shrugged. The answer was perfectly obvious to her. "Become friends with it. Let it hang around with you. Talk to it. Fall in love with it, and give it a chance to fall in love with you. Let it take care of you, because that's one thing dogs like to do, and they're good at it."

"Oh sure. Do I have to feed it, or will it feed me? Will it fill my water bowl? Will it make my bed, clean my house, do the shopping, and cook me meals? Come on, Alice. No dog is so dumb that it would want to take on all that no-fun stuff."

The dog shifted slightly, sat down on the floor as if aware this was going to be a long negotiation. He didn't look worried.

"I don't want it, Alice." As soon as she said the words, Rose felt horribly guilty. As if she'd deliberately hurt the animal's feelings, inflicted a wound that would heal slowly, if ever. She tried to sound less truculent, trying to explain to the animal why she was being so negative. "How am I supposed to fit a dog into my life?"

"What sort of fitting do you have to do?"

"Okay, for example, I am about to meet Lance for coffee in the Mizpah. I can't leave the dog here in my store, can I? What if he runs amok, eats all the fabric, chews the shoes? I don't know this animal. You don't know him either."

"He's seven years old, and that's quite a bit past the puppy stage. I seriously doubt he'll go on a rampage."

"You don't know that."

"No," Alice conceded, her eyes concerned—eyes that looked much like the dog's eyes. Same yellowish color, same persistence, same patience. "So why not take the dog with you into the Mizpah?"

"Are you joking?"

"No. Not at all. You think Ned Stalks would object? Or that the Mizpah is such a classy place, anyone would dare protest? Or perhaps you're worried that Noodle will become a heavy drinker like all the other boring barflies that haunt the place."

"Why is he called Noodle? That's the stupidest name for a dog I've ever heard."

"Who knows why?" Alice shrugged her slender shoulders. "It's the moniker he came with."

"So what am I supposed to do? Stand out in the

middle of Main Street calling out, 'Noodle, Noodle, come here'? People will think I've lost my mind. *I'll* think I've lost my mind."

Alice was laughing. Which, although she desperately wanted to remain sulky and negative, made Rose laugh too. As for Noodle, having heard his name, he got to his feet, slowly moved over to Rose's side, and gazed up at her beseechingly.

"What am I supposed to do with him when I go into Reno on business?"

"Bring him back to my house for a doggie holiday. He gets along perfectly well with all the millions of other dogs I've rescued."

Rose sighed deeply. Glared down at Noodle. "I'm not saying 'yes' to you, okay? This is a test run for both of us. If this doesn't work out, then you'll be back on Alice's doorstep, pronto. Got it?"

The dog wagged its long corkscrew tail in response.

"Does he have a leash, at least?"

"Sure does." Alice stood, reached into her pocket, and pulled one out. Then pointed to the large plastic bag she'd brought. "That's enough dog kibble for a few days. He'll need a big bowl for fresh water. Anyway, since you're meeting up with Lance, having Noodle with you will win you brownie points with the guy. After all, he's a veterinarian, isn't he?"

Rose sighed again. Then attached the leash to Noodle's collar, marched into the front room, and hung the Back in Five Minutes sign on her shop door.

****

"Yes," said Lance. "I met Noodle last week when Alice called me and asked me to give him his shots.

He's in excellent health. He also has enough shepherd in him to make him a good protector."

Rose, perched on a barstool at the counter, peeked at Noodle. He was sitting calmly at her feet. "Maybe," she said. "Alice calls it fang support. But he's still ugly. You must admit he's ugly."

"Well, he's no classic beauty," Lance conceded.

"Not dog show material, that's for certain."

"How many of us are?"

"True. I'd never win a poodle prize."

"Seriously, Rose, when you get used to him, you'll think he's gorgeous."

"Oh, sure. Eventually, I might start looking like him, too. Don't people always end up looking like their dogs? If my ears become as pointy as his, I'll never be able to wear earrings again. Goodbye glamour."

Lance chortled. "We'll have to wait and see."

He might be right about Noodle's looks, she thought begrudgingly. She had already decided the creature was fairly decent-looking after all, although she'd been a dog owner—and a reluctant dog owner, at that—for around half an hour. Yet, there was something to be said for having a warm furry thing sitting by your side, looking up at you from time to time, checking out that things were fine. She plucked a peanut out of the cup on the counter, bent down, offered it to Noodle. After sniffing it cautiously with his large rubbery nose, he took the nut with infinite gentleness.

Lance smiled. "You're lucky. I think you've got yourself a good deal."

"It wasn't a deal. Alice bullied me into it."

"She's pretty good at that kind of thing."

A high resounding and infinitely painful squeal

came from the back room of the Mizpah and destroyed the peace of a perfectly normal day.

"The Old Boy's Band." Rose grimaced. "Ned lets them rehearse in the back room from time to time. They're right behind that wooden partition because nobody, especially not their wives, will have them rehearsing at home."

"Why not?"

"Because they're awful."

Another resounding squeal confirmed her words, and Lance squeezed his eyes closed as if in pain. Even Noodle flinched. Which was when the door of the Mizpah opened and let in a blast of cold desert air and cheery-faced, smart-stepping Tracey Kipps.

His face lit up when he saw Rose. "Saw the five minutes sign on the door of your shop and figured you'd be in here for an hour or two."

Tracey Kipps, an old flame from way back when: lighthearted, completely superficial, and a lot of fun. He came up to Rose, pulled her off the barstool and into his arms for a big hug. Then released her gently, looked over at Lance. The two men began sizing each other up, competing bull style. Rose smothered a giggle, then introduced them, mentioning that Lance was a veterinarian, and Tracey an insurance man. "Both of you spend your time covering every single mile of the desert."

The barflies lined up along the counter gawped at the three of them with evident interest. Yes, here was the sort of scene they liked to witness: once again, Rose was playing fast and easy with two rivals (or so they thought). What a new juicy piece of local news to take home to their long-suffering partners for further perusal.

However, instead of giving them some really spicy grist for their gossip mills, both Lance and Tracey showed each other polite civility, then began talking about the area they covered, the people they both might know. Rose smiled. She loved male company. She looked down at Noodle—another male. Alert, his ears twisting this way and that, he was watching the two men with interest. Checking them out? Gauging the amount of testosterone in the air?

Which is when the door opened again.

Rose glanced over, and her breath caught. Jonah. She hadn't heard from him since the night of the concert, a week ago. She wasn't certain she'd ever hear from him again. Yet here he was. Her heart warmed. She'd missed him, and the memory of being with him had lingered, keeping her warm over the intervening days.

What was he doing here in Blake's Folly today? No one could be here by pure chance? Of course, that didn't mean he was looking for her, did it? He had mentioned that he would be spending quite a bit of time out at the old Winterback Mine. Perhaps he was here in the Mizpah for some warmth, a coffee, and a meal. But she knew she was trying to fool herself—just so she wouldn't feel disappointed if she were mistaken.

Slowly, casually, in that wonderful sauntering way of his, he joined the three of them. Rose introduced the three men. Again Lance and Tracey sized up the competition—except they couldn't know that Jonah wasn't competition, Rose reminded herself.

Her eyes ran over the craggy lines of his face. How delectable he looked, available or not available. Her heart sighed. If only she had the right to lean over and kiss that lovely mouth of his. Or touch him, right there, on the shoulder of his black leather jacket.

"Jonah is also covering every inch of the desert," she said, hoping her voice sounded calm and controlled, that it didn't betray those last steamy thoughts of hers. "The difference is, that as a geologist, he covers what's underground, the stuff that no one else normally sees."

The barflies were fascinated now. Some forgot to sip their beers. Rose with three male admirers! This was too much. Didn't this promise a shoot-out, one as violent and exciting as those that had taken place in this same room back in the town's glorious old days? Back when mustached gamblers, gold miners, cowboys with quick tempers and nervous trigger fingers all sought the favors of the sloe-eyed good-time girls.

"How about if we all sit down at a table. Get comfortable," she suggested. Get out of everyone's hearing. She noted how crushed the barflies were. As usual, they'd soon be moving in closer so as not to miss a word.

She slid into the booth on her right; Jonah was beside her, on her left. She could smell the natural scent of him, the hint of cool fresh air, sand, and something else: a subtle but sexy musk. Her hand was resting on the seat, right next to his thigh, not touching him, but itching to do so. Casually, she moved it closer, until she could feel his heat in her fingers. No one would notice, would they? Certainly not Jonah, who wouldn't allow himself to think of her in a sensual way like that.

She looked up, saw Lance staring at her strangely. Had he noticed? The look was gone in the flash of a second. She had to be careful. If she couldn't fool

101

herself as far as her feelings for Jonah went, she had to keep fooling everyone else, Jonah included. She forced herself to concentrate on the conversation.

The three men continued talking, and to the on-lookers' great disappointment, all seemed to be relaxed. Rose kept the conversational ball rolling, asking questions here and there, introducing new topics when the last one threatened to get stale, or when silences became heavy, yet managing to reveal little about herself. It was a refined technique, one not given to everyone. Except Jonah had noticed, all right. He'd made that perfectly clear the day they'd sat in the Dew Drop Inn. If she weren't mistaken, he was also the sort of man who would dig around until he'd dragged out all her little secrets.

The long sliding door separating the Mizpah's main room from the back area screeched open, and the Old Boys, brandishing two electric guitars, an electric banjo, and an electric violin, made their appearance. The painful-sounding rehearsal was at an end, and the Boys' whistles needed wetting. In their colorful cowboy boots and jingling spurs, they sashayed up to the bar. Sly Grimes, lead singer, eyed Rose and her three male admirers. Then smirked. His mother was going to like this bit of information.

"How-dee, Rose," he called out. "How'y'all doo-win-n-n."

Rose forced back a giggle. Sly had invented and perfected (if such a word could be used in this case) an accent that he imagined was a savant mélange of Far West and the Ozarks. It was, of course, nothing of the sort: most of the time, the man was almost incomprehensible.

"Hi, Sly. Getting ready for a concert?"

"Juss practicin' uhp for the ann-yull Get-Together."

Inwardly, she sighed. Although the Get-Together was on a Saturday night and the Old Boy's Band was the worst group in the Western hemisphere, if she deliberately stayed away from that notorious social occasion, she would become a complete social outcast in Blake's Folly and over a vast portion of the surrounding area. Then what would she do? Eliminate conversation with the cranky local population, and there were only rattlers, gopher snakes, and giant hairy scorpions for miles around. Chats with those creatures would make for a pretty lonely life.

"You-all gonna sang wiff us one day?" Sly had moved in closer to the table and, beer in hand, was staring straight at her.

Rose gaped. "What?"

"You-all gonna sang wiff th' Boys one day?"

Oh hell. Why was he asking her that? She scratched around in her mind for a change of subject, saw all three men, Lance, Tracey, and Jonah, had stopped talking and were listening to the exchange, such as it was, with undue interest.

"No," she said shortly. Then, turning her back to Sly, she asked Lance, "So Noodle doesn't need any other shots this year?"

The tactic didn't work. Sly possessed a one-track mind, and at this very moment, it had a runaway locomotive rolling down its steep gradient. He turned to the others in the room. "Rose used-ta-be a music sty-ar. In th' old days."

This had to stop. Immediately. Rose grabbed her

103

handbag and pulled out the keys to Second Hand Rose. "Duty calls. I have to get back to the shop." As she hoped, Lance, Tracey, and Jonah all rose.

"Have to hit the road again," said Tracey.

"Ditto," echoed Lance, shrugging himself into his jacket.

Jonah said nothing, but he was watching her with a little too much curiosity. Well, she could deflect his interest, couldn't she? Wasn't she good at that?

"Are you off to the Winterback, Jonah?" she asked when they were outside the Mizpah.

He nodded. "I'll walk back to the shop with you. That's where I left my car."

The other men waved goodbye. Then the three of them were alone, she, Jonah, and Noodle, crossing State Street, passing the abandoned shacks on Main.

Jonah looked down at Noodle, trotting passively beside them. "I didn't know you had a dog."

"I didn't until about an hour ago. I was bullied into taking him. My so-called friend Alice claims I have to have one in the shop to protect me from who knows what. In reality, she rescued this one and needed to find a home for him. She already has too many dogs to feed."

"Sounds like a good idea to me. For all three of you."

"I've done fine on my own without a dog up until now." She observed Noodle who seemed perfectly happy to follow along beside her, as if he'd known her for the last five million years or so. "I'll need to develop some pretty sharp powers of divination if I want to find out what breed he is, though." Not that she cared. She simply didn't want Jonah questioning her about what Sly had said back in the Mizpah. Jonah was a musician, for heaven's sake. He might have picked up on the words "sang" and "music sty-ar."

"What difference does it make?"

"I agree, actually. It makes no difference whatsoever. Certainly it makes no difference to Noodle. He accepts what he is, no questions asked. He probably never looks at himself in mirrors or contemplates an identity crisis."

"Noodle? Is that his name?"

"Not my fault. That's the moniker he came with. Tell me, Jonah, what are you doing in Blake's Folly today?"

"I was passing through. And I wondered if you felt like taking time off one day next week to go look at some Paiute petroglyphs with me. Don't say yes if you aren't interested. I won't be offended."

She stopped in her tracks and beamed up at him, her heart thumping with pleasure. "I'd really and truly love to go look at petroglyphs with you."

"How about Tuesday?"

"Great. I'll ask Lucy to watch the shop."

His returning grin was warm and wonderful. She was absolutely certain that he was as pleased as she was.

"How about Noodle? Can he come too? Believe it or not, I can sense he's really into rock carvings."

Chapter Ten: Petroglyphs

He had arranged to pick her up at ten o'clock on Tuesday morning; it was a long drive out to the Paiute reservation in the northeast. She was already waiting for him, dressed as he'd suggested, in thick socks, walking boots, her warm jacket, woolly hat, scarf, and mittens.

"I feel like I'm ready for an expedition to Antarctica."

He nodded. "It can be cold out where we're going, and there's always a nasty wind slipping in between the hills."

She peered at him from under her lashes. "Still, I prefer a glamour girl image to this Yeti look."

Was she fishing? Of course, she was. His mouth slanted into a wide grin. "You'd be an uncommonly attractive Yeti." It was true. Her natural beauty would shine out no matter what she did. Funny how beautiful people became when you cared about them, and he certainly did care about her. She had touched him in some deep way, and that emotion had nothing to do with her considerable powers of seduction. "Don't worry. You don't need glamour girl trappings, not with your looks, you don't. You're pretty gorgeous."

"Oh," she said. "Thanks." Her cheeks flushed a soft pink.

"You're welcome." The blush intrigued him. Was

she embarrassed? Surely, she was used to compliments. She was the sort of woman who received them all the time. Perhaps it all depended on who gave them…

She held out a plastic bowl and a wool blanket. "The bowl is for Noodle because he might get thirsty. The cover is for the car seat so that his nails won't leave scratch marks on it."

"Have you looked at the back seat of my car? You should see what I normally put there: measuring equipment, rocks, canisters, fossils, bones, and the occasional sandwich."

"Still…" She peeked inside and smirked. "Okay, point taken. It's just that most men and their cars…well…you know what I mean."

"I know exactly what you mean," he concurred. "To me, a car is not an extension of my ego. It's merely a means of transportation and a work tool."

"How nice to hear something so sane. Well, let's see if Noodle likes cars and road transport."

The animal didn't hesitate when Jonah opened the back door. He leapt onto the seat, sat, and seemed perfectly at ease in the usual wet-nosed canine way.

"How were Noodle's first nights in his new home? How's he settling in?" Jonah asked as they began heading down toward the main highway.

"Him? He's fine," Rose scoffed. "I'm the nervous wreck, fussing around, making sure he's comfortable, that he likes his chow, that he's not too bored but having a good time. I know it's silly, because he goes along with everything, following me like a faithful hound should, waiting politely when I'm busy, never chewing up what he shouldn't, and never barking. At around nine every evening, he lets me know he's feeling sleepy, and then he flops down on his blanket and snores away. All hell could break loose, but he wouldn't notice." She turned, observed Noodle speculatively. "In fact, I'm not convinced that he has any watchdog instincts at all. He has a truly relaxed, remarkably Zen attitude to life."

But, then again, so did she, which was why she was so easy to be with. She and Noodle seemed like the perfect match, as far as dog and dog owner went. "Have you ever had a dog before? Aside from wanting to please him, you seem to take Noodle's presence in stride."

"No. Never. I really wanted a dog when I was a kid, but no way I was ever going to get one, not with my kind of mother. However, I pass quite a bit of time around dogs, these days. You don't have a choice when you're friends with Alice Treemont. She spends her life collecting strays. Half the residents of Blake's Folly have been bullied into adopting at least one of her orphans. Now, I've fallen into the same trap."

The morning light was bleak, and the road, a pale straight ribbon, seemed to roll out endlessly between tumbled rocks and drab winter scrub. Conversation was intermittent, yet the long silences were comfortable, as if there were a feeling of complicity between them— and much understanding. He was relieved. He could be entertained by light chatter in small doses, but he'd always found too much of it irritating. Which seemed to be the way she felt too: easy with quiet; perfectly at ease with her own thoughts.

They stopped for an early lunch in a roadside cafe where wind had covered windows with red dust, and country music whined on about ruined love, broken hearts, and lonesome nights.

"How much farther are the petroglyphs?" she asked.

"Worried?"

She grinned. "Not in the least. I trust you implicitly."

Of course, she could trust him, he knew that. Still, her answer made him feel strangely proud. He couldn't have asked for anything more. "Good." He noticed the huskiness in his own voice. "Because I'm taking you to a rather lonely location normal tourists never see."

Which was easy enough to believe. As they drove on, there was more scrub, more desolation, more bleakness. It was a silent, lonely landscape, seemingly uninhabited; and other than the odd branch shivering in the chill breeze, there was no visible movement. It was good to know she trusted him.

"How desolate this area must have seemed to the pioneers who crossed it in their covered wagons," she said. "They never knew how many days' walk lay before them, or how far away good fresh water was, or if this emptiness would ever come to an end."

"And all that happened not so long ago." He turned onto a barely visible gravel track running between bleached hills, one easily overlooked.

"How do you know about this place?"

"I used to come out here with my grandfather. To him, the petroglyphs were almost sacred."

"Don't you think that might have stirred your imagination, inspired your career choice?"

"Yes, that's probably true. My grandfather passed down to me his love of empty spaces and windswept sites. He also taught me to respect the physical world via the Northern Paiute belief in *puha*, the power that is an equal part of all elements, plants, animals, and humans."

They bumped along until further progress was impossible. Then Jonah pulled to one side, turned off the engine. "From now on, we're on foot."

Almost as if he understood the comment, Noodle stood, wagged his tail gently. He was more than ready for a good run and the chance to snuffle around this unknown terrain.

It was a long walk between the hills, and as Jonah had predicted, the needle-sharp wind was punishing. Progressing over the stony pathway wasn't simple, either. He watched Rose. Like on that bitterly cold day when he'd taken her out to the Winterback Mine, she didn't look as though she minded either the rough going or the chilling, dust-filled gusts. She was a good sport, and he valued that, but he wondered where all the resilience came from. The golden hair, soft mouth, and petite figure didn't speak of the great outdoors or rough adventure.

His eyes picked out a narrow opening between high boulders on the left. Yes, this was the turning he was looking for. Reaching out, he caught her elbow in his hand. "We're almost there, but be careful. Some of these stones are loose. Spraining an ankle would be pretty easy to do." Twenty feet along, the passage took an abrupt turn. Suddenly, they were out in the open, in an area of jagged hills, where every surface was covered in geometric patterns, concentric rings, and tree-shaped etchings.

"How wonderful!" Rose turned slowly, took in every zigzag, each swirl. Her enthusiasm was sincere;

he could see that by her shining eyes, hear it in the warmth of her voice.

"I never, not even for one single minute, imagined a place like this existed. Tell me all about petroglyphs. I know nothing at all—other than the fact that they're incredibly old."

"Well, few scientists agree on their exact age. People used to believe they were a mere three thousand years old, but we now know that the early North Americans made them around 15,000 years ago. Look over there, at those mountains in the distance. Do you see the carved terraces? Those were made by the waves of an ancient lake that once covered this entire area. The petroglyphs were created during a long, dry period when the lake temporarily vanished."

"Do we know what the symbols signify?"

"No." He shrugged. "Researchers have been arguing for years about their meaning. One thing we do all agree on is they're definitely not a form of writing."

The wind stiffened, became an icy tentacle that worked its way between the tightest seams. Despite her many layers of clothing, Rose must be freezing, although he knew by now that she would never complain. She had a delightful character, a complicated one, too. But standing out here in the bitingly raw air, he wouldn't penetrate the deep mystery that was Rose Badger.

"Okay. Excursion's over. What we need now is a warm car to take us back to civilization and a good dinner." And the chance to get the answers to a few questions, he added to himself.

****

On the way back to Blake's Folly, they returned to

the Dew Drop Inn with its kitsch Wild West decor—wagon wheels, stirrups, cowbells, lassos—and satisfying soup. This was the same Dew Drop Inn where her mother had waitressed all those years ago, Rose mused. After quite a few detours, her own life had brought her back here, too. Totally relaxed and happy, she cupped her hands around her warm bowl, savored the heat. It had been a lovely day, different, exciting. "Thank you for taking me to see the rock carvings."

"You're welcome." Those heart-searing crinkles were back.

"Tell me more about your Paiute grandfather," she prompted.

He didn't answer, and the crinkles vanished. "Do you remember what I said the last time we were here?"

She shook her head. "What are you referring to?" Although she realized what was coming.

"About how good you are at asking questions and avoiding talking about yourself."

"Ah." It wasn't an answer, not by a long shot. Carefully, she settled her bowl on its dish and waited.

"Which makes me curious."

"Oh, there's not a lot to tell." Which was the wrong thing to say, and she knew it. He knew it too. She could see that by the amused flash in his eyes.

"The other day in the Mizpah, that man with the strange accent said something about you singing…if I interpreted what he said correctly. What was he referring to?"

"I thought you'd probably pick up on what bigmouth Sly Grimes said."

"And?"

"Oh, it was nothing, really. I used to sing in a few

places." She shrugged, as if it had been of no importance at all. She was dying to ask him a question, deflect his curiosity, yet she knew he'd understood her tactic too well now, and that he'd persist until he received a few answers, ones that would satisfy his ever-inquiring mind.

"What sort of singing?"

"Not the sort of singing that would interest you." She played with her spoon, turning it this way and that on the tabletop.

"How about if you let me be the judge of that?"

"How about if I don't really want to talk about those days? How about if all that isn't important?"

"Fine." He leaned back in his seat.

She was being unfair, and she knew it, too. In a way, she owed him information. Back in Reno, after the concert, he had confided in her. He had told her about things that had been close to his heart so she could understand him, see how he functioned. Didn't that mean she also owed him a few confidences?

"All right." She put down the spoon and met his gaze squarely. Why not tell the truth? The past was behind her. She had changed her life. "You want to know what I'm hiding? Here goes. Be prepared, because this isn't some interesting, cute story about singing at weddings and family parties. It's a whole planet away from your life, your world of university, and studies, and refinement. I mean, look at you, a geologist, a man with a doctorate. Dr. Jonah Livingstone." A man who, despite the worn leather jacket and jeans, oozed sophistication, education.

"Go on," he prompted.

"Go on? Fine. Look at me. No doctorate, no

university, not much education."

He was actually chuckling softly. "I'm looking, all right. I see a beautiful, wonderfully intelligent woman."

"Oh, come on." She pushed away the compliments. "I followed in my mother's footsteps, quit school when I was sixteen."

"Who told you that education means intelligence? I meet highly educated people all the time, but quite a few of them are still jerks."

She stared.

"Okay. I'm listening. Why did you quit school at sixteen?"

"I didn't have much choice. You said your grandfather influenced you. For me, it was my grandparents, because my mother didn't raise me. She was too busy changing lovers and getting drunk in Reno's casinos."

"So you lived with your grandparents?"

"On and off. Sometimes my mother would breeze into my life, take me out of school, bring me to Reno for a while, then decide I was a burden and send me back to my maternal grandparents."

"They lived in Blake's Folly?"

"In the old Red Nag Saloon. My great-great-grandfather built it way back when, and it was passed down from one generation to the next. It was a great place to live in. There were so many rooms, forgotten corners, and scary nooks, the sort of stuff kids love."

"It's still standing?"

"Of course it is. It's on State Street. You've probably passed it hundreds of times."

"Maybe. I didn't notice it."

"I could show it to you if you'd like?" Why was

she feeling so shy?

"I'd like that."

She felt like kicking herself. Why would he want to see another local wreck? "You don't have to be polite. The place doesn't look like much of anything, these days. Not since it's been in my mother's hands."

"I think we've had part of this conversation before." His eyes twinkled. "I'm not being polite. I'm interested, okay?"

"Okay." Now what? How much should she reveal? She sat there, silent, listening to the clatter of cutlery, the clack of stacking plates, the ever-complaining whine of country music. All around, perfectly normal-looking people sat at other tables in the restaurant, talking, laughing, outwardly content. What sort of lives did they have? Was anything really as seamless and trouble free as it seemed?

Jonah was waiting. "Continue. Tell me more."

Why was she hesitating? Hadn't she said she trusted him? Yes, she had. So, it wasn't because she thought he would broadcast any information she gave him over the whole state of Nevada. It was something else altogether.

She took a deep breath. "When I was almost fifteen, my grandfather passed away—he was a wonderful man who taught me so much. I was heartbroken. So was my grandmother, and she died less than a year later. That's when my mother swept back into town. She'd inherited the Red Nag, and she started selling off every single mirror, table, rug, and drinking glass in the place. When it was all gone, she locked the door, told me I had to make my own way in the world, and went back to Reno. So, suddenly, I was homeless…"

"What about your paternal grandparents?"

"I spent lots of time with them when I was a kid, but my paternal grandmother was dead by then, and her husband, my step-grandfather, had passed away years earlier."

"So what did you do?"

"I took the one option open to me—the one that sounded good, that sounded like making dreams come true. I hitched to San Francisco, crashed in people's apartments, hung around the streets and the bars until I managed to create a career of sorts—singing with a few rock bands. Finally, at eighteen, I got married to Billy Bunt, guitar player, rock star hopeful."

"So that's what Sly Grimes was referring to?"

"More or less. My maternal grandmother had taught me how to sing. Before coming to Blake's Folly and marrying my grandfather, Polina had been a professional singer in Russia, then in Reno. Because she loved music so much, she was quite determined to give me, as well as my mother, good musical training. She was a strict teacher in the old-fashioned way, so I learned to adapt to pretty well anything."

"You sang with your husband?"

Her mouth twisted with mockery. "Billy had a group. He was lead guitar, I sang, Jim was the drummer, BooBoo played bass, Lazy Hal, the keyboard. We went wherever we could find work, traveled all around the country."

"No children?"

"Nope. I've never wanted any. I lack the gene that gives most women that maternal urge, and that's pretty fortunate. How could I have raised a kid decently with that sort of lifestyle?"

"Did you enjoy the itinerant life?"

"Enjoy?" She looked out of the restaurant window, to where day was fading. That time seemed so long ago. It had been another life, a different world. "It was fun at first. I was running wild; I was a rebel. I thought I was smarter than everyone else, which wasn't true, of course. It was the stupid bravado that goes along with being too young to analyze anything and getting a swelled head with all the applause from people who didn't know any better. What I loved, though, were the gigs that lasted all night, the strange sensation you get when you emerge into the bright blinding light of morning, half high from the music, half spaced from fatigue."

"I know the feeling you're talking about."

"Yes, since you're also a musician, I imagine you do." She met his eyes squarely. "That was the good side of it. Those were the early years…until Billy got involved in the drug scene. At first, he was a small dealer and making enough money to keep himself supplied. Then, he became a man with a big habit. Life was hell. I was terrified of him, and I was terrified to leave. He followed me everywhere, never left me alone for a minute. He said he'd kill me if I abandoned him. I didn't want to take the chance he'd do that."

She expected Jonah's expression of disgust. The tightened lips. The rejection. Those reactions didn't come. He was only waiting for the rest of the story.

"Before that, when we could make money playing music, we lived in cheap accommodation or in lower end motels. Now, there was no more money for rent, so we slept in cars and squats, went out panhandling when there was no chance of working anymore because Billy and BooBoo were too far gone. When we got too hungry, we lived on what was stolen from supermarkets. We didn't care about risks. We didn't care about much of anything by then. Then there was all the other stuff too—the dicey, sometimes disgusting characters you meet in squalid squats, everyone down on their luck, nobody with any dreams left." She stopped.

His expression was still mild, uncritical.

"Well?" she challenged. "So now what do you have to say? You see why I don't relish talking about those days? Why I don't enjoy pointing out how lousy my choices were compared to yours?"

"What happened to your husband?"

"Billy? He died. Of an overdose. I woke up one morning, and there he was, lying on the floor of the squat."

"That must have been…" He stopped.

She felt defiant, not ashamed, and she wanted neither pity nor commiseration. "It was a relief, that's what. I can't tell you how much of a relief it was. I don't care if that makes me sound like a rotten person. I was thrilled, because Billy would never be able to threaten me again, or terrify me, or manipulate me. That lousy part of my life was over."

"So you came back to Blake's Folly?"

"Not right away. I stuck it out in San Francisco. Cleaned myself up, rooted out the people I'd once known, and got singing gigs again—nothing glorious, no acclaim, no wild applause. Restaurants, entertainment bars. A few weddings. Without Billy, I could meet decent musicians, the ones who were still hopeful, who were trying to do things in life."

"I never heard of Billy Bunt or his rock group. How did Sly Grimes know about you?"

"Pure chance. Some years ago, he also left Blake's Folly and came to San Francisco, tried to break into the entertainment business. He'd didn't succeed, because he was too inexperienced, and too gentle for that competitive dog-eat-dog music scene. But he happened to see one of our performances one night, and thought that as a hometown girl, I'd help him up the glittery ladder to stardom. He never found out how badly he'd misjudged the situation."

"Were you any good as a rock group?"

She had to laugh. "Nope. We were pretty mediocre. Neither Billy, nor Lazy Hal, nor Jim, nor BooBoo had originality. They'd copied what everyone else had done. I didn't use my voice the way my grandmother taught me to do either—as a real singer. I dressed myself in wild clothes, screamed out lyrics, and watched the crowd jiggle around in a trance. Looking back on it all, I can honestly say that we were good at making a lot of really irritating noise and being pests."

"How did you get back to Blake's Folly?"

"I woke up one morning and had a kind of epiphany. I knew the sort of singing I was doing in clubs and restaurants wasn't interesting, even if it brought in some money. I didn't want to live in the city any longer. More importantly, I didn't believe in myself anymore. So I came back to the only solid roots I'd ever known. In Blake's Folly, I had the peace and quiet to explore what positive life choices I could make."

"And you opened a secondhand clothing store?"

She hesitated. The shop, Second Hand Rose,

wasn't really what it seemed to be, but she didn't have to tell Jonah everything, did she? Vintage clothes, her success in that field...well, that was business, and another part of her life altogether. She was so used to keeping secrets, it was easy to sidetrack. "I'd made a vow to never, ever, sing rock music again. I'm not saying it's bad. It was a bad choice for me. I'd never again do bland moneymaking singing either. I had been selling my soul for too long."

He reached across the table, took her hand in his, a totally unexpected gesture. The gesture of a friend? She searched his face. What did he think of her now? He was smiling, the corners of his mouth rippled into those lovely folds, his dark eyes warm.

****

He stopped the car in front of her shop.

"Do you want to come in for a coffee before setting out again?" she asked as he opened the back door for Noodle.

"I can't. I have to get back to Reno." It was an excuse, and he knew why he needed one. He wanted to spend the rest of the evening in her warmth, glory in the bright light she exuded. In her strength. If he followed her into her territory, the temptation would be too great. He ached to fold her into his arms, feel her mouth, and knew he couldn't. Friendship didn't allow for gestures like that. Friendship? The hell with that! He wanted to make love with her, spend the night beside her. "Thanks for telling me your story."

"You aren't disgusted?"

"Disgusted? Are you serious? Disgusted by what? A glimpse into another world?" He had to reassure her, tell her he would never condemn her for a life so different from his own. For choices made when fate hands you a weak deal.

"Look, I was always the good boy, the perfect kid, the model student. I went to university because my family expected me to do that. I studied geology because I'd always had a rock collection. It never dawned on me to do anything else, probably because— although the history of my people is a glimpse into sheer hell—my parents made sure that family life was stable. The sort of life you led was out of the question for me. I'd never have dared to question anything, leave home, be a rock singer, or live in a squat. I was too obedient, and probably too scared, to make rebellious choices."

In the dark, he could see she didn't really believe him.

Again, he reached out, took her hand in his. It was the one intimate gesture he could allow himself, but he needed to touch her. Feel her warmth. "I admire you. You have to believe me." He released her fingers. Raised his hand, caressed the softness of her cheek. Traced her lips with his fingertips. Then, with a mighty effort, he dropped his hand.

"Good night, Rose."

"Good night, Jonah." Her voice was soft temptation.

He forced himself to look away, get back into the car, turn the key in the ignition, drive down toward the highway, head for city lights.

Chapter Eleven: Costa Rica

To Rose, her shop seemed about as calm as a Nevada train station during the silver boom days. Roy Palmer had made himself comfortable in a fragile-looking settee that had surely been created in an era when men were less brawny and their body language less casual. His long legs in their cowboy boots were stretched out before him, and his vast, muscular arms were thrown over the back of that unfortunate piece of furniture. Any minute now, it looked as though the elegant remnant of another era would finally give up the ghost.

Leaning against the jewelry counter, perfectly at ease, and looking like he was more than willing to become a permanent fixture, was Tracey Kipps. And Ma Handy, unchallenged Queen of Gossip in Blake's Folly (beating Jane Grimes for that title), was happily ensconced in the large velvet armchair and listening intently to the conversation, her eyes greedily flicking from one man to the other.

Not that there was anything of gossip value in what either man was saying: Roy was vaunting the pleasure of ice fishing up near the Canadian border; Tracey was talking about the holiday he was planning in Costa Rica. As for Noodle, far from being the fang support Alice had promised, instead of growling when each person had walked through the door, he'd given all a warm welcome and a few wet kisses. Now he was perfectly at ease, sitting on the floor, watching, and wagging his tail.

Rose tapped her foot with impatience. Sitting on the worktable in the back room was the large cardboard box that had been delivered minutes before Roy, the first uninvited visitor, had shown up. She knew what was inside: bolts of fabric, survivors from the thirties, forties, and fifties. Little did anyone imagine there was still so much of it around: beautiful cottons, lace, velvet, and luxuriant silks. Her suppliers knew her taste, knew what she was looking for. Each time another delivery arrived, she was as excited as a kid at Christmas.

Except the last thing she could do was open the box, look inside, not with this crowd in the shop. Okay, the men would never notice anything was amiss, but Ma Handy had sharp little ultrasound eyes, and she was bound to ask questions: why did Rose need all the fabric? What was she planning to do with it?

How could she explain? No one in Blake's Folly knew she designed the lovely dresses hanging in the shop. No one suspected she did. Certainly, no one imagined she ran a discreet yet successful business via the Internet. Why *would* they? There were no visible signs of wealth in her life.

After the cost of the fabric, the salaries to her seamstresses, she didn't make a lot of money. She'd never wanted to. The designing was what she loved; and this thick-walled building of solid brick was hers because she'd bought it with her own money—money made thanks to her creativity. She loved her bright, old-fashioned workroom with its long windows running the length of one wall. She delighted in her study with its many reference books, her lovely square bedroom with its silky counterpane and old furniture. These things were all she needed in life. These, and the freedom to go into Reno on Saturday evenings. She didn't want luxury.

All in all, she was perfectly satisfied with her life and her activities. The round, good feeling of satisfaction was there every single morning when she woke up. Even now, despite…Despite what? A niggling little doubt. A strange restlessness. A longing for something as yet nameless. That came from where? From her attraction to Jonah? *Ridiculous.* From her one-sided attraction. Yes, that was more like it. Had Jonah ever showed her he wanted more than friendship?

Roy pulled in those long legs of his, stood. Finally. "Well, Rose, nice seeing you again." His tone was casual, but his eyes betrayed him. Obviously, he had hoped to find her alone so he could invite her out. She knew Roy would never extend an invitation in front of others: he was too reserved for that. Well, she'd be hearing from him before too long. He'd call, invite her to lunch, or dinner. If she accepted, it would be pleasant enough, she knew it would be. Pleasant, not exciting. Not stimulating. She would ask the right questions to get him talking about himself, his life, his world, and time would pass smoothly. Roy wouldn't pry; Roy didn't care about her past, or her ideas.

Not like Jonah. Jonah was different in that way. How many people actually asked you questions and listened to the answers? Not many. Not many at all. Other than the gossips…

Ma Handy was the next to leave, and she did so

with obvious regret—outside, the sun was glaring with noon fervor, and that meant it was close to lunchtime. No doubt, Pa Handy was already seated at the kitchen table, table napkin tied, bib-like, around his neck, sharp little knife and pronged fork clutched in his meaty paws. Only Tracey lingered, observing her, his eyes amused.

"You'd like Costa Rica," he said, his voice warm, full of seductive promise.

Rose nodded. "I might well. Who knows? There are many places I might like in the world, but I don't think I'm much of a traveler."

"How do you know?"

"Because I can't be bothered making the effort to go see those places. Not these days. I'm perfectly happy with my life here, as narrow as that sounds."

Tracey's smile faded slightly. "How about coming with me?"

"Coming with you? Where? To Costa Rica?"

"Why not? Tropical rain forest, sun, beaches, a warm sea. It's a world away from Nevada. Doesn't it sound appealing?"

"Yes, of course. In a way…"

"Three weeks of paradise." He came up to her, kissed her gently on the cheek. The kiss of an ex-lover who was hoping to edge his way back into the picture. "Think about it."

She nodded. "Okay, I will. But as I said, I don't think that I'm adventurous, and I'd rather—"

"Think *seriously* about it, Rose," he interrupted. "I'd love to have you come with me."

Silently, she watched him. Then he waved, opened the door, went out into the chill, and drove off.

Tracey asking her to go traveling with him? How strange. Their brief relationship had never been serious. Always easy, always casual, they had remained on good terms after it had ended, meeting occasionally for drinks, a meal. Then, two years ago, they'd lost touch. Why had he appeared in her life again? Why was he inviting her to go with him?

She liked Tracey, although she knew she could never fall in love with him. Why not? Because the dazzle was missing, the wonderful spark that comes along with mental stimulation, that turns a relationship into magic. Still, she thought about the invitation. What if she seized the chance, went with him, had a fun holiday? A carefree change of scene?

What about Jonah? What would he say about it? Would he be jealous? Would he be disappointed in her? Jonah was so different from all the other men she knew—although all the times she'd spent with him, sitting, talking, learning about things she didn't know, were entirely innocent. Still, the warmth she felt toward him, the undeniable attraction, those were hard to deny. He was the sort of man she loved having in her life…would always love having near her. He was a man she might fall in love with—if she let herself. Yes, she admitted that now, even though the thought didn't make her any happier. If there could be a future?

She shook herself. What sort of future? At the moment, Jonah was a man with a big responsibility: Marina. A commitment like that could go on for years and years. Besides, Jonah had never shown her he wanted more than friendship; he'd never hinted at it.

What about her? She needed to be free, didn't she? Isn't that what she'd always said? Free to make choices, free to take Tracey up on his offer. So, why not do that? Why not bask under a tropical sun, sip something delicious laced with coconut milk? Jonah had nothing to say about it. He'd be as unavailable as ever, tucked, snug as a bug in a rug, into his apartment with Marina. Rose shoved down the sudden, unexpected, spike of jealousy mixed with resentment.

****

Here he was, roaring down the ruined highway, heading for Blake's Folly. *Again.* Skirting deep potholes, stirring up a prairie dust storm. Damn! Why the hell couldn't he keep away from the place? *The power of Rose Badger? Boy, do you have it bad.* But how he enjoyed doing things with her, talking with her, watching her. He couldn't get her out of his mind, and more than anything, he hoped she was in the same confused state. *Besotted idiot.* Jerking to a halt in front of Second Hand Rose, he stepped out onto the gritty road and slammed the car door behind him.

As soon as the bell above the door jangled, Noodle appeared, a tail-wagging, fuzzy, hospitality greeter. And here was Rose, leaving the back room, a sharp cutter in one hand.

She stared. "Jonah." Her head tilted to one side, and a faint flush slipped over her cheeks.

"Am I interrupting something?"

"Good heavens, no. I wasn't expecting *you*. I've been besieged by visitors all morning, and none of them were people I particularly wanted to see, but you..." Stopping abruptly, she flushed a delightful pink.

What had she been about to say? That she was happy he was here? Jonah hoped so. He was certainly pleased to have her standing there, right in front of him.

A pleasure for the eye. "I thought I'd drop by, see if you were free to show me the Red Nag, then to go have some lunch."

Her expression changed to something akin to doubt. "You actually meant that the other day? You really want to see the place?"

"As I said." Why mention it was an excuse? Being with her again was all that mattered. *Play it cool, idiot.*

Rose took in his worn jeans, his scuffed boots, the tired leather jacket. "Jonah…it's pretty dusty in there. Several decades' worth of dust, actually."

He chortled. "I can survive that. I spend most of my life up to my neck in dust that's millions of years old."

Rose grinned back.

He waited while she disappeared to change into a pair of jeans and pull on sturdy boots. Then locking the shop door, they set out, walking down rutted, weedy, perfectly empty Main Street, turning into equally rutted, equally weedy, equally empty State Street. Halfway down the block, Rose stopped.

"Here she is, in all her glory."

Yes, of course. He'd passed this way many times, but he had never singled out the ruined building, not with all these other derelict businesses along the road. Two stories high in weathered wood, the tall false front had once made it look imposing, and a wooden sidewalk had allowed customers to shake off the unpaved road's ubiquitous dirt. The words Red Nag Saloon had all but disappeared from the signboard, rubbed transparent by more than a century's sun and abrasive sand. He surveyed the front door, barred by a heavy chain and rusty padlock. "No key?"

"Nope. But that's never kept me away." Her wink was wicked. "We can get in through the rear of the building."

They rounded an old barbershop, its striped pole hanging askew, found themselves in a backyard wasteland of old planks, two abandoned cars, and what surely had been, once upon a time, a wooden wagon. With a competence apparently honed by long practice, Rose sidestepped treacherous chunks of metal, straddled old tires, and wove a light-footed path around heaped junk, so long discarded, there was no telling what purpose it might have served. Stopping at a boarded window, she reached under the wooden frame and pushed at a slat of wood. As easily as that, the tired planks gave way with a complaining squeal.

"I'm impressed. You do this often?"

She turned to him, eyes twinkling. "Not so much these days, but I used to sneak in and spend time here in the Nag when I first came back to town—after all, this had been my real home when I was a kid. I hoped my mother would let me buy the place from her. Of course, she had no intention of doing so. She preferred letting it fall to pieces. I finally put all my energy into the building that's now Second Hand Rose."

"What strange behavior. Why would she let something that belonged to her ancestors fall down?"

"Pure laziness, that's one reason. But perhaps it's more complicated than that. Maybe this place points to all her lost chances, to her bad choices."

"Punishing the building as a way of punishing herself?"

"That sounds about right."

Inside, his nose was assailed by the quiet, musty

J. Arlene Culiner

odor of an old house long abandoned, of other scents, too, more feral, those of wild creatures who seek shelter in forgotten places. Aside from a long, sculpted mahogany bar running down the left side of the room, the former saloon was empty. Faded wallpaper hung in strips; broad floor planks were thirsty-looking.

"For my grandparents, the most important room was the one where they lived. It's upstairs. Come, I'll show you, although you'll have to use your imagination. Every object it once contained has been scattered, and its exotic elegance only exists in my memory."

They climbed a staircase that still felt solid despite the faint sag in the center of each step, and entered another room, square and symmetrical. "It was so beautiful once, or at least to me it was. Isn't it sad, the lack of permanence? I've always felt that remarkable places should be kept for posterity and the joy of other generations, but life isn't like that."

"That's how things have always been. New generations erase the old."

"You're right." She turned full circle, looking at the bare walls. "Polina, my grandmother, told me that her own village was destroyed by war. Houses that were hundreds of years old were wiped off the face of the earth in a day or two. Even if she hadn't managed to leave the Soviet Union, she could never have gone back. She'd seen what war did to places, the shattered buildings, dead animals, houses split in half with, by a strange quirk of fate, a table still standing in one corner, a picture hanging on one remaining wall. Or, in the middle of a devastated field, an oven with a pot still sitting on the top."

"Testimony to an innocent, unsuspecting moment," he murmured.

"Exactly that. And because Polina could never return to the past, she recreated what she'd once known right in here, thousands of miles away from her roots."

"This became a little corner of Russia."

Rose went to the far corner. "Along here was a table, and over there was another. Next to that was an old-fashioned credenza, and everything was covered by long, fringed, hand-embroidered cloths. Right by the window, was a big unwieldy copper-potted rubber plant, and everywhere were knickknacks, paperweights, vases, ashtrays, and three black elephants, remarkably heavy—made of what? Ebony? Possibly stone. I loved them, they were so smooth and majestic. Where did they come from? What happened to them?"

Silently, he watched as she moved about the room, so light on her feet, she almost danced, her gestures so eloquent that long gone objects almost became visible. He loved the way her golden hair caught the light streaming through the window; he loved the timbre of her voice.

"There were rag rugs on the floors, a red and white one here, another with blue and green and bright yellow stripes near the door. And on every wooden chair, every armchair, there were crocheted cushions. My grandmother said that in Russian cottages, there were always traditional icons and old photos on the walls. Since she was a refugee and had none, she covered every wall in this room with paintings and embroidered panels."

"It sounds as though there were a great many things all in this one smallish space."

"True. There were. But it wasn't messy or crowded. Everything had its own place, and it all came together and formed a complete picture."

"A museum of the soul?"

She stared at him, her pale blue eyes wide. "That's it. And now it's all gone."

"All interiors are lost eventually, Rose. In every building, when it changes hands, furniture is removed, sold, or destroyed. Walls are redecorated or they're knocked down. Windows are enlarged, doors are filled in. All the importance of a house belongs to the person who inhabits it."

"You sound as sentimental as I do."

He couldn't stop his sudden shout of laughter. He leaned against the doorframe. "During the hundreds of years that your ancestors were filling their lovely wooden houses with embroidery, paintings, and icons, mine were semi-nomadic. We lived in temporary willow-framed huts in the summer, or cone-shaped wickiups, winter dwellings covered with reeds, sagebrush, branches, brush, bark, dirt, and grass. We had woven baskets coated with pine pitch for cooking and carrying water, and like our sleeping mats, when they wore out, they were simply chucked away, or burnt and replaced."

"We're a whole cultural world away from each other," she mused.

Then, yes, not now, he thought, but didn't say. Each moment he spent in Rose's company gave him the strange feeling that they were so similar…although he hadn't the faintest idea where that crazy idea came from.

Chapter Twelve: Marina

Eleven thirty in the evening. The pump of rock music, the sound of laughter filtered out into the hallway as Jonah unlocked the door of the apartment. Marina was entertaining again. His heart sank. After tonight's grueling rehearsal, it would be wonderful to have an hour or two of complete silence. Second best would be a glass of wine and calm conversation. Not that Marina was interested in calm. Or silence. Or in his music. Marina had always been a party girl, vivacious, in need of crowds, friends, noise, and lighthearted interaction. Irreconcilable opposites, that's what they were.

He carried his cello into the room he used as an office. Stretched his tired muscles—did non-musicians realize how tiring playing was? Probably not. He went to the window, looked out into the night, out onto the twinkling city lights. Thought of Rose…as he usually did these days…her family history, the life she had lived. For the thousandth time, he compared it to his own tame existence: geology, the world of books, knowledge. He admired her, he really did, although he suspected it would be hard to convince her of that.

He would have loved to have been free enough to run wild when he was younger, but his sense of responsibility had kept his feet firmly glued to the ground. He had needed to succeed; he had wanted his family to be proud of him, and geology had been the perfect choice. It brought him back to the ancestral lands of his heritage, and to the countryside he loved with a deep, inexplicable passion. Rose seemed to share his passion for the local beauty. That was something they shared. What were the other things? Music, perhaps. She had seemed to love his music, and that was important to him. Very important.

The door opened behind him.

"Jonah?"

He turned. Marina stood there, drink in hand. He almost hissed with exasperation. "You shouldn't be drinking."

She held her glass in the air, and her voice was mocking. "Party time, Jonah. Relax, for once. Have some fun."

"You are on medication," he insisted. "Medication that doesn't mix with alcohol."

"Oh, cut it out. I'm allowed to have some fun, too."

All fun and no self-discipline, that was Marina, all right. Which was why they were both locked into this situation.

She lifted her glass in a toast. "Cheers, Jonah. Why don't you come into the living room, join the crowd? Laney is here, and Todd. A few others."

"I'm not in a party mood, Marina."

"Spoil sport." She looked coy, batted her eyelashes. It was mere show.

"How did your talk with Buddy go today?"

Marina's face closed down. "No talk."

"What do you mean, no talk?"

"I cancelled."

"You cancelled?" He stared, unable—or

unwilling—to believe his ears.

"I'm not ready."

The same old excuse. Except that it had worn tissue thin. Refusing to return to the working world, to take up her contacts at the university, to return to the job that remained open for her, meant she would still be in his apartment and still dependent on him.

He wanted one thing. He wanted Marina to stand on her own two feet, be a strong independent woman again. A woman who loved her work, the intricacies of law, and the judicial system, who kept up her many contacts in the outside world. A woman whose conversation had been stimulating.

He wanted—needed—to be free. Because of Rose? Because it was getting harder and harder to resist her, to keep things on a platonic level?

How did Rose really see him? As a man who was too weak to make a move, to get out of a situation that was a burden to him? Worse yet, he knew it wasn't right to end one relationship so that he could jump into another. That would make everything sordid, somehow. It would cost him his self-respect, perhaps Rose's respect, too. He couldn't take that chance.

No, what he needed was independence, breathing space. Silence. Solitude. When he had those things, he'd be free to examine the other possibilities. Explore, more deeply, the feelings he had for her. He knew what they were at the moment: longing and fascination. Admiration. What if they became something else?

What about Rose? He didn't doubt for a minute that she had many admirers. Hadn't he already met some of them? He hated the idea of the other men in her life. His male gut instinct was to stake his claim, tell the world she was his own. At the same time, he wondered if he wanted a permanent relationship with anyone again. He wasn't sure he did. One thing was clear: he and Rose had to talk, be honest with each other, discover how each felt. He couldn't risk losing her, losing the closeness they had created.

He contemplated Marina, still standing in the doorway, swaying slightly, her eyes challenging but slightly unfocused.

"You are ready," he murmured. "You know you are. If you're ready for parties, for friends and the social whirl, then you're ready to start your life again. This situation was only a temporary solution. I need my freedom back, Marina."

Marina stared. Without aggression. With disappointment. And sorrow. Did she think he would go to her, comfort her, tell her things were fine, and apologize for being so brutal? He wouldn't. Not again. Never again.

And, quite suddenly, he found a solution. A way to solve the problem. A reasonable way. One that would be less painful for her. Why hadn't he thought of it before? Why had he been so sluggish?

"There's a simple way we can do this, Marina. You don't need upheaval, and I'm willing to do whatever I can to make the change easy for you. But you'll have to start working again; you have to join the world. I'll help you, but this situation won't continue."

Her face was tragic; her eyes filled with sudden tears. Still, he wouldn't compromise, not again. He'd done what he could, and now it was up to her.

He looked at Marina with sympathy. "It's time, babe. It's time."

Chapter Thirteen: Secrets

"Rose?"

Perfect silence greeted him. She must be in here somewhere. The shop door was open, the till unguarded, although if it contained any money was anyone's guess: he'd never seen this place packed with customers. Once again, he wondered how Rose survived on the sales made here.

"Rose?" he called again.

Not a sound.

Then, as usual, Noodle ambled out of the back room, his claws tapping on the wooden floor. Fierce watchdog that he was, he wagged his curly tail with rapture and headed straight toward Jonah for a pat. "Fang protection," he muttered as he rubbed the dog between his pointy ears. "At least tell me where Rose is."

Noodle didn't answer, of course. Jonah crossed to the back room and poked his head through the doorway. Stopped, surprised. He hadn't expected to see another area of this size. It was obviously a former workshop of some sort, perhaps once used for light manufacturing. Broad windows along one long wall let in late afternoon's glancing light. There were wooden worktables, one long, two smaller, all topped by bolts of flowing cloth. Yes, it still was a workshop, evidently. A clothing workshop? On a rack along one wall, several dresses hung, luxuriant fabrics in muted ruby and pearly gray velvet.

"Rose? Are you here?"

She appeared suddenly, framed in a doorway to the left, a long sheaf of paper in her arms.

Her mouth curved upward, her eyes warmed. "What a lovely surprise." Then the softness disappeared, and her eyes swept the room. She looked what? Embarrassed? Wary? As if she'd been caught out doing something she shouldn't have—or wouldn't like him to know about.

"I called out. Obviously, you didn't hear me. Noodle did, though. He came out on high alert, threatened me with all his fangs. I talked him out of a show of violence, but it wasn't easy."

Her smile returned. "I'll bet that happened." Despite the smile, she was still looking uncomfortable.

"Isn't it dangerous leaving your door open so that people can wander into the shop without your hearing them?"

"Perhaps. It doesn't happen all that often. I was in another back room packing some fabric and…" The sentence dribbled into nothing.

"What is all of this?" He waved his arm, a gesture that took in the wooden tables, the bolts of cloth, a sewing machine, chalks, papers, many pairs of scissors, and two long rulers.

She hesitated. Deciding on whether to let him into the secret? Another part of her life? Then, resigned, she placed the paper she was carrying on a table. "Okay. Come on in, I'll show you."

He followed her into another room, smaller, cozier, an untidy library of sorts, where books were piled, pell-mell and without obvious order, along broad shelves.

He inspected them: art books, books on fashion, clothing design, some of them older, from the middle of the last century.

She sat down at a round wooden table. "I design clothes," she said simply. "After Billy's death, when I was living in San Francisco and singing in bars, I decided that I wanted another sort of life for myself. I had always loved the old-fashioned clothes from the thirties, forties, and fifties, the ones that I'd seen in the magazines in my paternal grandmother's house—she was an authentic fashion fanatic, a fancy lady and a pack rat, so she never threw anything out. I did a high school equivalency program and then studied costume design."

He pulled out a chair and sat, too. "But you aren't a costume designer."

"No, of course not. How far would that get me in Blake's Folly? By the time I knew I intended to return here, to Nevada, I realized I also needed a business loophole in order to survive."

He watched her curiously. "Why have you never mentioned this? Why have you been so secretive about what you do?"

"Because I cheat," she said. "I'm famous for my vintage dresses, although they aren't vintage at all. They are one of a kind, and the styles are authentic. Since I use fabrics from the forties and fifties to make them, people believe—or let's say they *like* to believe—that the clothes I sell are antiques. Which they aren't."

"Where do you sell them? Not here in Blake's Folly."

Her moue was rueful. "Well, I don't do a roaring business out here, although I do have customers who will drive out and fall in love with a dress that is perfect for them. However, most of my clients are in San Francisco and Los Angeles."

"Doesn't anyone know about this? Don't people ask questions?"

"Funny you should mention that." She leaned forward, her elbows on the table. "You're an exception, but haven't you ever noticed that people rarely ask questions? They like to talk about themselves. They'll tell you their most intimate secrets, yet they don't notice half the things that are going on around them."

"What do people say when they see the cloth, the tables, the tape measures and scissors?"

"Only two people are allowed to come into my workroom. One is Lucy Barnes who works in the shop and is fairly clueless, because her one interest in life is looking for and photographing spiders. The other is my friend Alice who studies snakes and writes articles about them for herpetology magazines. Neither one knows anything about clothes or fashion, and I doubt that they think this room with these books on design is interesting."

"And you do well?"

"I don't make a fortune, and I don't want to either. I made enough to buy this disused furniture workshop." One hand waved dismissively. "Of course, it came cheap. Not too many people are looking to buy abandoned buildings in semi-ghost towns. The locals all came up trumps, though. They helped me fix the place up, replace glass panes, redo the electrical wiring, put in plumbing, repair smashed plaster, and paint the walls, so that helped a lot. These days, I can also pay my seamstresses decent wages."

"Your seamstresses?"

Looking down, she fiddled uneasily with a small box of sewing pins on the table. "I don't know if I can tell you this. It isn't information I should give out. I've never talked about it to anyone."

"Okay. If it's a big, dark secret, don't tell me. I'm being nosy."

"It's not that I don't trust you…"

"It's okay. Forget I asked."

"No." Pushing away the pin box, her eyes met his. "I'll tell you some of it. My seamstresses live in Reno. They are women who are illegal immigrants. They're terrified they'll be expelled from the country and separated from their children who were either born here, or who are all receiving a good education. You see, schooling is something that wasn't available to them in rural Mexico. One of the women is also hiding from a violent husband."

The light in his head clicked on. "And employing them is illegal."

Her chin tilted rebelliously. "Yes, it is."

He nodded. She trusted him with this information. They were making progress, the two of them. They had already come a long way. Further than she might have realized.

He reached out and cupped her defiant little chin, let his thumb caress her lovely mouth. Briefly. An intimate gesture, he knew. One he couldn't resist. He wanted—needed—to touch her. She felt the same way, he could see that by the softened expression, the sudden flutter of her lids.

"I'll keep your secret, don't worry. At the moment, however, I would like to know one other thing."

"And that is?"

"Do you have any more of them?"

"Any more of what?"

"Secrets."

"Oh." She looked uncomfortable again. "Perhaps."

He felt like roaring with laughter. "Okay. I can wait."

****

Tracey was seated in a booth in the Mizpah, chatting comfortably with Roy Palmer. Neither Roy nor Tracey seemed in the least surprised to see her arrive with Jonah, and it was perfectly normal to join them at their table. Besides, Rose knew all her men were more than happy to spend time talking with each other, and that she was often an excuse for them to meet up.

And in the next minute, the door opened, and here was Lance Potter.

He came up to their table, observed the three men sitting with her. "Like bears around a honeypot," he joked, his eyes twinkling.

The comment didn't escape Mick Fletcher's ears. Shaggy-haired and sharp-fanged, beer bottle in hand, Mick was a fixture along the Mizpah's mahogany bar. Known for her caustic tongue, she wasn't about to sheathe it in velvet now.

"Or flies around a corpse," she called from the counter.

There was perfect silence.

Rose looked over at the woman, her eyes calm. "Something you'd know all about, right, Mick?"

Mick harrumphed, then turned her back on them

142

all. Rose knew what the woman meant. She also knew that, all appearances to the contrary, Mick wasn't a vicious person. It was drink that made her scrappy. Underneath, there was a heart of gold—although that sweet side rarely appeared unless there was an emergency of some sort.

"Actually, Mick is referring to what she considers the shadier part of Blake's Folly history," Rose said.

Tracey was evidently amused. "What shady side was that?"

She looked from one man to the other. What did she have to hide? She wasn't ashamed of her background, of her paternal grandmother's story. She didn't give a fig for other people's condemnation, and she heartily disliked hypocrisy. Wasn't this local history? A bit of insider information about life in the old days in Blake's Folly? A nice, juicy segment.

"She's referring to the brothels, of course. Everyone knows that, in the old days, there were houses of pleasure all over Nevada, particularly in areas like this, where the male population outnumbered the female. It was a lonely life, being out in the wasteland, panning for gold, trudging over empty space and hoping to find silver, working hard in the mines, or hustling and rustling, ranching on poor soil and barely surviving. Towns like Blake's Folly were an oasis for such lonely men, and what could be more appealing than an oasis within an oasis, where the decor was welcoming, luxurious, and alcohol was served by scantily clad women."

Tracey grinned. "You're making brothels sound quite appealing."

"I suppose I am, in a way. Of course, I know that

there were different categories of brothels. Some were sordid, horrid, vulgar places, with rooms off the bar for convenience and speed. There were others, too. Madam Lacey's on State Street was a sumptuous palace—well, for the desert, it was—with exotic plants, red draperies, plush sofas, low lights. One room was decorated like a ship's cabin, another was called the Turkish room."

"What happened to Madam Lacey's?"

"The building? It burnt down long ago."

"You seem to know a lot about it." Lance's voice was lazy.

"Of course I do. My paternal grandmother worked in Madam Lacey's before she married my step-grandfather and became respectable." She paused, looked over at Mick Fletcher who was still standing up at the bar and, despite having her back to them all, listening with great concentration.

Rose raised her voice to make sure the woman heard all she was about to say. "That's what happened to most of the ladies who worked in the brothels. They eventually married local men, became respectable housewives, and had families. Some of their descendants have no idea what they got up to. But the others—" She kept her voice clear and high. "They know perfectly well, although they'd rather die than admit it."

Mick lifted her bottle to her mouth, took a slug, as if she hadn't heard a word. But she had. The bright red flush on her neck told all.

What did Jonah think about her now, Rose wondered? Would he consider such a background a stigma? She peeped in his direction. He didn't look shocked, or offended. The man was unflappable.

"Did your grandmother talk to you about that time?"

Rose thought about the woman who had been so kind to her, who had tried to make up for her father's quick disappearance. "Sometimes, yes. When I was old enough to understand her story, she told me about the brothel, and she gave me the feeling that she missed those days. That she'd somehow turned the life of a sex worker into a fond memory, or at least a picturesque one. She described nights when a little orchestra and an excellent banjo player would come to play in the main room; and she said there was real solidarity between all the girls who worked there. There were also certain clients she always looked forward to seeing."

"In other words," Jonah said, "the picture she painted was anything but sordid."

Rose nodded. What a lovely, intelligent man he was.

To make certain that particular topic of conversation was closed, Lance stood, moved his chair until it effectively cut off Mick Fletcher's view of their table. Then he sat, smiled at Roy: "So how are things going out your way?"

The ploy worked. Roy was relieved that this subject was one he could whole-heartedly expand upon. "Last fall, I installed a frost-free dispenser to keep the animals supplied with water in freezing weather. We have a water heater for the chickens too, but the major problem is frozen eggs. If they freeze solid, the shells crack and they have to be used right away." With that, he launched into a rather colorless and detailed description of wintering out on his ranch.

Rose tried not to burst out laughing, and she threw

Lance a grateful look. Although the subject was tediously dull for everyone except Roy, attention had been diverted away from her.

"Winter poses additional problems for all of us," said Tracey when he finally managed to get a word in edgewise. "Which is why I'll be happy to get away to a warmer climate for a few weeks. Costa Rican sun, beaches, good food, here I come."

"Costa Rica?" Temporarily thwarted, Roy's brow furrowed.

"That's right." Tracey looked smug. "I think I've convinced Rose to join me."

Roy raised his eyebrows, so stunned by the news, he completely forgot about ranching. "Is that so…"

"Ah," said Lance.

Jonah said nothing. Rose could feel his eyes on her, but she couldn't bring herself to look at him. What did it matter to him, anyway? Yet, she felt terribly uncomfortable, as though she'd broken faith in some strange way.

Chapter Fourteen: The Loft

"So this is it?" Pete Lucas, lawyer by day, baroque recorder player by passion, and Jonah's close friend, looked around the loft. Heaped cardboard boxes, a minimum of furniture, suitcases, a stack of wood planks, scattered tools, and two toolboxes took up one third of the space. The rest was airy and empty. "This place is enormous."

"No kidding. It will be a great rehearsal space for all of us."

"That, it certainly will be. How about if we celebrate your moving in here with a mini-concert?"

"I was hoping you'd suggest that. I can't think of a better way to do a housewarming."

"We'll have to call the others, choose a date that's right for everyone."

"Absolutely."

"What's great is that with the solidity of this loft, no neighbors will complain about the noise, even here, in the middle of Reno."

"True. Old industrial buildings like this one are totally soundproof." Jonah took in the large space. "I love the thickness of these solid brick walls. The complete silence."

Pete watched him curiously. "That's something that would drive most people crazy. How about you? How will it feel to be living on your own again?"

Amused, Jonah looked his friend squarely in the eye. "How do you think it will feel? This is what I've wanted for so long. I've missed being alone. At the moment, I feel great, and I'm just moving in."

"And Marina?"

"Marina's fine. She's a pretty good sport, at heart." He knew he could say that with complete sincerity and not a little relief. "She knows I'll be always be there for her if she really needs me—but she can't become a burden again. She also understands that I'm not her partner."

"She accepts that?"

"She does now," Jonah said quietly, and knew it was true. "I need to be alone."

Pete's smile was sly. "Really? Do you? And who was that beautiful little blonde you left with after our concert?"

"Ah. Rose Badger. You saw her, did you?"

"Couldn't miss her."

"No, that would be hard for any man to do," Jonah acknowledged. What could he say about Rose? "She's a lovely person. Kind, intelligent, and exciting." And desirable, incredibly desirable. A woman he ached to be with, to take in his arms, to make love with.

Pete waggled his eyebrows. "And?"

Jonah grinned back at his buddy. "Rose and I are friends." Although the words didn't sound right to his own ears. Not anymore. "As long as Marina was living in my apartment, I felt uncomfortable about seeing another woman. And yes, I know that sounds silly. It sounds ridiculous to my own ears. Somehow, I felt I had a bargain to uphold—if I wasn't one hundred percent sure what the bargain was."

"And now?"

"Who knows?" He certainly didn't. Who was Rose? With her deep secrets and her hidden feelings, she was not unlike the will-o'-the-wisp, that ghostly flickering figure seen by lone travelers. Seductive, irresistible, receding when approached, luring all away from safe paths.

"Rose is a woman who attracts men wherever she goes, and that's what she loves. She always has male admirers hanging around her, calling her, inviting her to dinner, or to travel to exotic countries with them. I fit perfectly into the mold. Whenever I'm with her, I feel like I'm part of the clamoring crowd. Interesting, special perhaps—but not *overwhelmingly* special, if you see what I mean. Not like a man she cherishes more than any other. It's not a flattering position to be in."

"I can imagine."

When Pete left, Jonah pulled out a chair from a chaotic pile of recently arrived possessions. Sat down, stretched out his legs. Despite the large windows, there was no noise from the street. Once, this area might have been a teeming manufacturing center; these days, traffic was scarce, and the factories had long since closed down. Many of the neighborhood's redbrick industrial buildings had been converted into attractive artist's lofts and elegant condominiums. In the spring, the bare trees outside his window would add a wonderful touch of green to the stark scene.

Jonah took a deep breath. This was it. This place belonged to him alone. The sense of freedom was heady. He was alone. Answerable to himself and no one else. Finally. It felt wonderful.

Chapter Fifteen: Saturday Evenings

Three weeks passed without seeing Jonah. He hadn't come through Blake's Folly. He'd called twice to see how she was, but the conversation had been light, almost impersonal. So why did that matter? Why was she so crushed? Because Jonah seemed to have decided that their outings and his visits to her were over? Because he was no longer interested in being with her?

Well, there were plenty of other men around, men who were more than happy to have her company, to pay her homage. Had he been shocked by her stories? By her secret life? She hadn't thought so at the time. Still, his absence had to be explained somehow. Was he annoyed because Tracey had said he was trying to convince her to travel to Costa Rica with him? If so, why hadn't Jonah asked her if she really planned on doing that? Perhaps it was something totally different: perhaps he had decided he was in love with Marina again.

Whatever it was, she wouldn't let herself mope any longer. She'd do the opposite. Seize life. Costa Rica? Okay, yes, she'd go with Tracey and stop brooding about an unavailable man. Imagine: twenty-one days in a tropical paradise. What fun! She thought of rain forests (although she'd never seen one), pictured herself wearing a sexy sundress and dipping a long silver spoon into some exotic fruity dish while Tracey's amused eyes watched her. There would be steamy sun, a warm sea, and much laughter. Tracey was always in a good mood. He was always ready for dancing, flirting, meeting new people, and dining out. Didn't sound at all bad, did it?

So why did the idea make her feel so miserable?

Insistent rapping on the shop door snapped her out of her reverie. She looked at the wall clock. Seven in the evening? Not a customer. Jonah? Her heart caught. The rapping continued, a harsh sound, like cut diamond on glass. No, definitely not him. Whoever it was, would smash the door's glass if they carried on like that for much longer.

"I'm coming!" She snapped on the table lamp in the shop and peered out into the night, her heart sinking when she recognized the lumpy form outside. Oh, no. Exactly what she didn't need. Fetching her key, she unlocked the door.

"Elsa. What are you doing here? Is something wrong?"

"A lot you care," Elsa muttered belligerently. Pushing past Rose, she entered the shop and looked around. Her beady, resentful eyes missed nothing: hats, shoes, clothes, the rich colors, and the glow of handcrafted jewelry in the glass case. "Doin' pretty good for yerself, aren't ya."

Rose closed the door and turned to her mother. "What is it you wanted, exactly? An inventory list?"

"Always ready with a smart mouth. Always thinking of yerself. Selfish, always been selfish."

Rose didn't bother answering. She could smell the waves of alcohol Elsa exuded, and she knew that any riposte would result in nothing short of a full-scale battle. All she could do was wait and see what the woman had come for: money for booze or cigarettes, most likely.

"You goin' into Reno?"

"Now?"

"Not now. Tomorrow? The day after that?"

"Why?" Although she knew what was coming.

"Cause I wanna ride in, that's why."

That was all she needed. A long trip with Elsa at her side, complaining her way through the miles, accusing her of neglect, of any emotional crime she could call to mind. What would she do with her once she got there?

"I can't go in anytime you want me to. I have a business to run. I drive in on Saturday afternoons and spend the night with friends. There's no room for another person." She shuddered at the idea of spending more time than necessary with the woman: Elsa's Reno trips were reserved for playing the slot machines and all-night drinking binges.

"Of course you'd say that. As I said, yuh always were selfish."

"Where would you spend the night?"

"Well, Miss Know-it-all, I'm not going to horn in on yer flashy life. Doan worry. I got my own friends."

"Fine."

"Sal. I'm meetin' Sal."

"Good for you."

"So I'm ridin' in and out with you?"

"Saturday afternoon. Be here at three o'clock. We'll head back to Blake's Folly on Sunday, at noon."

"I'll be here, all right. Doan leave without me."

To her infinite relief, Elsa, swaying tipsily, headed

for the door and was swallowed up by night.

Rose looked down at Noodle. He was staring at her with the usual pure adoration. Having him in her life did make it more fun. He was a lousy watchdog, that was clear to everyone, but he was a sure ally, one who would never judge her, nag her, break her heart, betray or disappoint her, or tell her she shouldn't be feeling the way she did.

When she was certain her mother wouldn't be staggering back down the road in her direction, she fetched her coat, slipped it on. After a visit as depressing as that one, only a decent glass of Chardonnay would make the life look less dreary. "Like mother, like daughter," she muttered grimly.

She was pulling on her gloves when the telephone rang.

"Rose?"

"Jonah." Pure joy swooped in, instantly banishing her dismal mood.

"I'm at the Mizpah. Lance is here, too. Do you want to join us?"

She sighed with relief. "I was on my way there."

She hadn't been forgotten after all. How nice!

****

Rose peered into the Mizpah before entering. The last thing she needed was finding Elsa here. Ten minutes of the woman went a long way. Yes, the coast was clear—as far as she could see. Unless Elsa was in the back room, or in a booth in some dark corner; the woman would never be opposed to one last tipple at the Mizpah before zigzagging her way back to her trailer and waiting paramour.

Lance and Jonah were standing together at the bar

as though they had been best chums ever since the Cenozoic era, when camels, mammoths, and giant ground sloths wandered through the deep forests once covering the county. With them was Jap Hardy, and he was holding forth, as usual, rolling out his much-rehashed monologue of how Blake's Folly had come into existence.

"Was a sheepherder out in the area, plenty of sheep around, back then. Digs himself a hole in the ground for his dutch oven and strikes some sort of peculiar rock. So, he takes a few samples of the rock into the supply store out on the old stage road, asks the proprietor if the rocks are worth anything. Old Tom Forbes, he don't know, so he says, 'nah, that ain't nothing.' So the sheepherder says, 'Ah hell, if it ain't worth nothing, I ain't gonna lug that crap around with me,' and leaves them rocks lying there on the counter. One day, three mining engineers come through, and see the stones, think they look plenny inneresting, so they take them into Reno, have them assayed. Discover they're silver.

"Of course, the sheepherder left the area long ago, so, without his help, they go out looking for the dutch oven hole. You can picture them, trackin' over every inch of the prairie, nothing out there but scrub, dust, dried animal bones, and strychnine poison water. But they kept at it. When they did find it, they dug down and found a vein of silver, four feet wide. In the end, years after the vein was worked out, people still came to Blake's Folly to scrape silver off mine walls. There was still enough to make them good money, too."

Rose approached the little group slowly, still peeking carefully into the shadows of booths lining the wall.

Jonah was watching her every movement. "You're looking strangely furtive."

"I'm avoiding my mother."

Lance laughed; Jonah chuckled.

She scrunched up her face with mock pain. "Okay, okay. I know how infantile that sounds, but I just got rid of the woman. She staggered over to the shop about fifteen minutes ago."

"Staggered?"

"Four sheets to the wind, as usual. She does make a habit of it." Rose wrinkled her nose. "Now, she wants to drive into Reno with me on Saturday."

"On Saturday? I thought you didn't do Saturdays," said Lance laconically.

"Really?" Jonah raised one quizzical eyebrow and turned to Lance. "What do you mean, she doesn't do them? She wipes them off the calendar? Crams everything into a six-day, Sunday to Friday, week?"

"It's her secret day. No one knows what she gets up to on Saturdays. Only that she isn't available. Ever."

"Aha. I was about to ask her to meet me this Saturday evening."

"She'll say no. She always does."

Exasperated, Rose threw both men the dirtiest look she could manage. "I'm not unavailable *every* Saturday. I intend to be here, in Blake's Folly, for the Get-Together, and that's two Saturdays away. Now, would you both please stop talking about me in the third person? I'm here, right in front of you. You can address me directly, and I can speak for myself."

"Except you don't. Not when it comes to Saturdays." Lance's voice was calm.

"Interesting." Jonah nodded. "I wonder what she

gets up to. A night at the roulette table?"

"Perhaps a rendezvous in some den of iniquity."

"Hmm. A secret husband and seven secret children?"

"A hidden lover?"

"A change of identity?"

"A second life as an investment banker?"

"Or as a lap dancer."

"A nude trapeze artist."

"Or a nude contortionist?"

"Okay, cut it out, both of you," Rose snapped. "You are about as much fun as my mother." To think she had been looking forward to seeing Jonah. Phooey.

"So?" Lance persisted. "Out with it. Spill the beans."

"Why is this so important?"

"To us?" Jonah asked, his voice soft. "Or to you?"

Damn. Now what? Tell all? Reveal her deepest secret? Well…why not? What did she really have to lose? "Okay. You win. Both of you. Which one of you has a piece of paper and a pen?"

Lance pulled both out of his pocket and slapped them down on the bar top.

Rose scribbled down an address. "If you feel that you *have* to know about my Saturday nights, that you have the *right* to question me about every single aspect of my life, then come here after eight o'clock in the evening. Push open the door and walk in."

She shoved the paper and pen back across the bar. Turned. Stormed out of the Mizpah.

Chapter Sixteen: The Russian Club

Jonah met Lance for a light supper in Lucky's before going to the address Rose had written down. He liked Lance, although he was a rival—of sorts. He liked his intelligence, enjoyed talking with him, hearing his point of view on politics, the world situation, and he was pretty certain Lance felt the same way about him. Then again, the men Rose collected around her all seemed to be nice guys, quite willing to accept the odd situation and the role of rival.

Perhaps they weren't rivals at all. As he'd told his friend Pete, Rose didn't seem to favor any one man over another. When they were together, they all seemed to be on equal standing as far as she was concerned, and none of them seemed to mind. Which wasn't a problem if your interest was merely friendly, superficial…and his definitely wasn't. By now, he knew—accepted—it was far more. Perhaps all her admirers felt the same way he did.

Except…she was apparently going away with Tracey to Costa Rica. He doubted they would sleep in separate rooms. They were going as lovers, weren't they? You never knew, where Rose was concerned. It wasn't the sort of question he could ask her, either.

"Do you have any idea of what's in store for us tonight?" Lance asked as they were putting on their coats.

"Not the slightest."

"It's a surprise of some kind, obviously."

"Knowing Rose, that's par for the course."

Lance nodded. "Under that sexy, gorgeous, exciting exterior, she's one pretty surprising person."

He smiled. "I'll second that."

In Lance's car, they drove out to an unpretentious area of small suburban houses, a few churches, and small shops. Then parked in front of an inauspicious building in cement and clapboard.

"Well, this seems to be the right address," said Jonah, peering out of the car window. The sign running along the front was written in (to him) undecipherable Cyrillic letters. Underneath, in smaller letters, were the words *The Russian Club*.

They stepped out into the street. Even here, he could hear music—was that an accordion? There were other sounds, too, and the faint tinkling of plucked strings. He and Lance went up the walkway to the wooden front door, pushed it open, and found themselves in a large hall, one filled with people sitting on chairs set out with no apparent order. Everyone was speaking loudly, too. In Russian? Well, it sounded like Russian to his ears. Did Rose also know the language? He'd never asked her. There were many things he had never had a chance to ask her. Yet. He felt like laughing aloud. What other mysterious world was she leading him into?

Up on a raised dais at the front of the room, a group of musicians were tuning instruments. What sort of instruments? He wasn't sure. Those triangular shapes had to be balalaikas in all their different sizes, from the tiniest, to a huge bass that could easily compete in size with his own cello. There was another stringed instrument too, round-bellied, lute-like. And three accordions.

"I wonder where Rose is," he shouted over the noise.

"Or if we'll ever find her. This place is crazy. What do you want to drink?" Lance grimaced. "Although, why am I asking? Probably the only thing the bar runs to is Russian vodka."

"Probably." This certainly wasn't a glamorous setting: the decoration was slap dash, unpretentious; people were dressed informally; the lighting was harsh. Yet, there was camaraderie, as well as excited anticipation, in the air.

Tuning finished, the musicians took their seats in one long line. The lights in the main hall dimmed, leaving the dais illuminated, and the music began…beautiful music, rippling, unfamiliar, almost archaic, yet powerfully urgent. In the dim light, he could see the pleasure on the faces of those in the audience. Some had begun swaying in time to these sounds that must be as familiar to them as they had been to their ancestors.

Then the music stopped. There was a hushed pause. When, it started again, it was wilder, faster. A woman stepped out onto the stage, and she was utterly beautiful. Her hair, wound into braids around her head, was held in place by a silver bandeau. She wore a full red skirt, a silvery embroidered vest over a full-sleeved white blouse. Around her neck, were ropes of colored beads.

Jonah gaped, transfixed. It was Rose, of course, yet it was another Rose altogether. This shining woman up on the stage was startlingly different from the one he knew. It was as if that were her rightful place, up there, moving sweetly to the wonderful music. Then she began to sing.

It was a sound he couldn't have imagined: her voice was high, flexible, and she played with an ancient-sounding melody, embellishing notes, lengthening vowels. Backing her were the musicians, and they sang the chorus with their rich male voices, a deep contrast to her soaring coloratura. Sometimes, the others in the room joined in, and when the music accelerated, three men in the audience stood—two were middle-aged, the third, grizzled—and with stamping, ecstatic kicking steps, began dancing, turning, advancing.

On went the music and the songs, the performance never flagging. It was so utterly different from his own music, yet equally thrilling. Then, almost too soon, it ended. The audience cheered, applauded, whistled. The main lights came on again, and Jonah looked over at Lance. The man's dazed expression had to be mirroring his own.

Silently, they watched the musicians leaving the stage and filtering in amongst the crowd. Rose, in the middle of one enthusiastic group, was embraced by a few of the older ladies. Others took her hands in theirs, and she smiled back with an easy grace. Eventually, she made her way across the room to where he waited with Lance.

"Well?" she asked, her eyes shining. "What do you both think?"

"You were wonderful," he said with absolute sincerity. "All of you were. What a superb voice you have."

She flushed with pleasure.

"Where did you learn to sing like that?" Lance asked.

"My grandmother taught me and my mother to sing in the authentic Russian way, in the high register some people call 'white sound.' Back in her day, singing was an everyday part of life. The songs weren't written down, because many villagers were illiterate, but the melodies and words were passed down from one generation to the next. My grandmother brought them to this country, and she sang to me every night before I fell asleep. That way, the music became part of me."

"What do the words mean?"

"A few songs describe the countryside, others are narratives about lost love, or personal struggles. The first was about a woman who goes to meet her lover, finds him with another woman, and so she lies down, dies. The last was quite different. It's the song of a woman who loves all the village men and doesn't care if she's frowned upon. However, if Vasily would say he loved her, she'd drop all the other men for him and—"

She stopped abruptly, swallowed, and Jonah could swear she flushed.

"Tell us about the instruments," said Lance, covering the awkward moment.

"The triangular stringed instruments are balalaikas. They have frets like guitars. The round-bellied, lute-like instrument is a domra, and it always plays the lead melody. Those accordions are Russian accordions, bayans, and they have the most wonderful range and purity of tone."

"I'd love to take a closer look at a balalaika," said

Jonah. "They have an incredible sound."

"I'll introduce you to Sergei. I'm sure he'll be thrilled to tell you all about them. They're his passion."

"Yes, I'd like that." Jonah gazed at her, at her radiant face. He was incredibly proud of her and so very pleased that she'd let him into this part of her world. Why hadn't she done it earlier? What was there to hide?

"This is where you always are on Saturday nights?" Lance asked.

"This is it. Of course, I don't always sing, and we don't always play music. Sometimes, I just meet with the other musicians in the early evening. We rehearse, learn new songs, and try new music. Or I come here for the conversation in Russian and the company."

"Why have you always kept this part of your life a secret?"

She frowned slightly. "I don't know, really. In the beginning, I had to hide my singing from my mother. I didn't want her to know about the Russian Club because I was afraid she'd show up and jinx everything."

"She's pretty good at that, I imagine," said Jonah.

Rose's mouth twisted wryly. "She does have that special ability. She comes to Reno quite often, so there's a gigantic risk involved. In fact, she's here in town right now, pumping her pension money into the slots and drinking herself into an aggressive stupor. Tomorrow morning, I get to drive her back to Blake's Folly, lucky me."

"Sounds like a pretty valid reason to keep this place a secret."

"Doesn't it." She smiled up at both men. "Other

than that, though, I don't have any convincing reason for not talking about this—other than the fact that I really do love having secrets."

****

The day was the usual dull winter gray. It had to be around twenty-six degrees out here. Last night, Jonah had said he wanted to show her something, but no amount of questioning revealed exactly what it was. Did that matter? No, it didn't. Before he and Lance had left, he had made a date with her for breakfast this morning, and that had been enough to keep her perfectly happy all night long.

She left Ana's and, following Jonah's directions, drove out to a part of Reno once zoned for industrial use. The Old Washoe Inn was a relic of the sort she thought had disappeared from the streets of Reno long ago. It was open, exactly as Jonah had said it would be, and breakfast sounded like a wonderful way to keep out the morning's sharp chill.

Jonah was already there, comfortably seated in a booth, his hands cupped around a mug of coffee. She also saw how his eyes lit up when he caught sight of her, and that warmed her more thoroughly than any warm meal could do. She slid into the booth.

"Hi."

"Hi, yourself."

She couldn't believe the tenderness in his voice either, unless she was dreaming. Wishing so hard that she mattered to Jonah that she actually believed she did. She ordered herself to calm down, stop living in a fantasy world. She looked around the room. Nothing seemed to have changed much in the last seventy years, or so. The same yellow tin ceiling that had probably been here in the good old days, the same old wooden tables, too. No doubt this was a popular hangout for tourists and locals who sought places with some authenticity, those far from the glare of casinos.

"Do you come here often?"

"Until recently, no."

"And recently?"

His eyes twinkled. He didn't answer her question. "Ready for breakfast?"

She nodded, although now that she was sitting opposite Jonah, her hunger seemed to have disappeared entirely. Her throat felt as dry as the desert floor—not that she'd let him know that. Not that she would let him know she was dying of curiosity, either. What did he want to show her? Why all the mystery? Why on earth did she hope, more than anything, it had something to do with her?

"Eggs, toast, and hash browns would be great." She'd force herself to eat all of it, too.

Jonah gave their orders to the waitress who had arrived with a pot of coffee.

"You still won't say what you're planning to show me?"

A smile flickered around the edges of his mouth, but he shook his head. "Still not saying."

The smile made her head spin and her stomach quiver. Boy, did she have it bad. It was getting harder and harder to hide her feelings, too. Her fingers longed to reach out, trace the smile, the crinkles, the line of his mouth. She ached with the desire to leap up, slide into the booth beside him, curl into him, and feel his thigh against hers.

A bad case of lust. Maybe a bad case of one-sided

lust. Although, she knew perfectly well it wasn't that.

He watched her, amused. "A penny for your thoughts."

She burst out laughing and met his eyes directly. "No way." Not in a million years. Never, would he know the way she felt about him. It was time she put her thoughts in order.

By the time the food arrived, her hunger had returned along with a good dose of common sense. *You're sitting here with a friend, remember? You don't lose your appetite when you're having breakfast with a good chum.* If she could keep her emotions in check, everything would be fine.

"Thank you for last night." Jonah's voice was soft.

She looked up, surprised. "Thanks? For what?"

"For opening the window to a world I didn't know about. A magic world. Here it was all the time, in the city I live in."

"Hey…ditto. For the music you introduced me to. To a world I knew nothing about."

"Music. A passion we both share." He shook his head, as if with wonderment. "Who would have guessed that, when I first walked into your store during a snowstorm?"

Their eyes locked, and her flesh tingled as if he'd actually touched her. Yes, music was a passion they shared. The only passion you share, she scolded herself. Although, as soon as her brain told her that, her heart felt less certain. The way he was looking at her, the softness in his voice. Certainly that meant something, didn't it?

"So, tell more about Reno's Russian community," he said.

And conversation became general, perfectly easy, and comfortable. Which reinforced her doubts. When the meal was over, Jonah paid, and they went back out into the windy street.

"Are we taking two cars or one?"

Jonah was smiling again, a mysterious smile, as though he had a big secret. "No car. We're crossing the street."

"To go where?" All she could see were ancient warehouses, the windswept street, and a few two-story buildings left over from the early 1900s.

"A special place. Come." He reached out and, linking her fingers through his own, led the way. The gesture of a friend? A friend reaching out to hold hands? His hand was warm, the skin was hard, the skin of a man who used his hands for work, for digging, for exploring.

The building he headed for was of red brick, with the high arched windows of an old industrial building—one long out of use. Still, it looked as though it were in decent shape, as if people cared about it. Jonah tapped in a code on the electronic keypad at the entry. He must come here often, she thought.

"What is this place?"

"It was a warehouse until around thirty years ago. Before that, it was a firehouse, and before that, a factory. Then someone decided it should be preserved as a historic building. These days, it's a loft condominium."

"Do you know someone who lives here?"

"I certainly do."

They climbed up to the second story, their footsteps ringing on the iron stairway. Jonah stopped before a heavy metal door, inserted a key.

"Shouldn't you knock first? Won't people mind us barging in like this?"

He didn't answer.

They stepped into a large loft apartment. The floors were wooden, and light spilled through a long row of multi-paned metal windows. Walls were the same red brick as the building's exterior, and thick ceiling beams were of white-painted steel.

"What do you think?" Jonah asked.

"What do I think? I think it's an absolutely wonderful place."

The furniture was sparse. There were a few cardboard boxes in one corner, right near a corner kitchen area. In another, someone was obviously building wooden bookshelves. Who did this space belong to? The question was on her lips, ready to be asked, when she noticed the cello lying on its elegant side, right next to a music stand. A cello?

She turned to Jonah. He was watching her with an unreadable expression.

"Is…is that your cello?"

He nodded. "It is."

"Who lives here?"

"I do."

"*You* do?" If this was where he lived, where was Marina? Why had he brought her here? "I thought—" Confused, she stopped, gathered her thoughts. "Look, you told me you lived in a high-rise condo."

"I did. Before. This is where I live now."

"Since when?"

"Since I bought this loft, signed the papers, then finished moving in last week."

"Moving in? Why…" She swallowed. "What happened? Where is Marina?"

"Marina lives in my old apartment. It was the easiest way of doing things, and the least upsetting for her. She didn't have to move out, didn't have to look for someplace else to live. She won't be alone either, because she'll have a roommate—a university colleague who's getting a divorce and needs a place to stay."

Rose stared at him. Took two steps, then sat down gingerly on the edge of a chair. Jonah was no longer living in the same apartment as Marina? He was free? Unattached? It was so hard to take in.

"I had no idea," she said vaguely. Why hadn't he said anything to her? Why hadn't he told her about the arrangement, or about buying this loft? "You didn't hint at any of this when we met."

His calm eyes met hers. "I intended to tell you about it that day when I came out to Blake's Folly, after we had lunch with Tracey, Roy, and Lance. What I had planned to do was ask you to come into Reno with me, take a look at this place. I had just found it, you see, and I wanted to know what you thought of it."

"What *I* thought of it?" Had that been important to him? "But you didn't. You didn't take me here."

"No, I didn't," he said, his voice steady. "Since Tracey announced you might be going to Costa Rica together, I realized you had other priorities."

Priorities? She gaped at him, wordlessly. She had considered accepting Tracey's invitation because she'd thought everything was so hopeless with Jonah. Had she been wrong? Did he want to be more than friends now that he was no longer with Marina?

"I've dreamt about living in this sort of place for years," he continued. "A place where I can play music until two in the morning without disturbing a soul. Where other musicians can join me for rehearsals. Where I can have silence, peace, breathing space."

No. He didn't want more than friendship with her. The meaning of his words was perfectly clear. He wanted his freedom. Freedom meant there was not much room for her in his life. *So what? You don't want a permanent relationship either, do you?* Making sure her smile was bright, that she sounded perfectly chirpy, she said, "Well, this calls for champagne, doesn't it? Will you be having a housewarming?"

"Quite definitely. It's all been arranged with my baroque chamber group, although it took a bit of negotiating so that everyone was free at the same time. The house warming will also be a concert, you see." He stopped, watched her closely. "Of course, you won't be around for it."

"Oh." She stood, but kept her voice as level as his. "Because I'm not invited?"

"Oh, of course you're invited. I'd really like you to be here. Very much. The party is in three weeks' time."

"And?"

"Didn't Tracey mention that you'll both be in Costa Rica by then?"

Chapter Seventeen: Revenge

Elsa snored loudly on the drive back to Blake's Folly. After a night passed in heaven only knew what depths of debauchery (and Rose definitely didn't want to know either), she was hardly up to the task of harassing her daughter. Rose was grateful for the (relative) silence, but the thoughts running through her head were hardly comforting.

It had been a shock seeing Jonah's loft. He was a free man again. That information should have made her happy, hopeful. It didn't. Why hadn't Jonah said anything to her? Why had he kept his life such a secret? *Because you protect yourself with secrets too.* True, but there were none of those left.

She had revealed everything to Jonah: the truth about her shop, her mother, her paternal grandmother, her own tawdry past, her secret life in the Russian Club. Why had Jonah been so insistent about knowing everything? Without secrets, she felt vulnerable. Secrets were her first line of defense. Secrets had been a way of surviving when she'd been married to Billy. Now, if she felt relieved that she had told Jonah everything, she also felt betrayed.

She'd always had male admirers, lovers, and hopefuls circling around her: what category could she put Jonah in? If he was a friend, how was she to interpret the way he watched her sometimes: with fascination, definite interest? Did he find her sexy? Desirable? She might never know. He'd kept his distance when living with Marina because he was an honorable man. He wasn't living with her now—the situation had changed some weeks ago, apparently—but he hadn't told her that. And he was still keeping his distance.

"Might as well face facts," she muttered to herself. "Jonah is not particularly attracted to me." He wasn't gay, she was fairly sure of that, but he'd never made a move to kiss her, take her in his arms. He'd never said that he hoped, one day, there could be more than friendship between them. Why had he kept coming around to see her? Why had he always been ready to propose an outing, an adventure? Why had he asked her to his concert? "Because he likes me, that's why." He liked her stories, liked hearing about her life. She amused him. Amusement was far from lust. Or love.

It was a hefty blow to her self-esteem—and an incredible disappointment. What was so unappealing about her? Was Marina so devastatingly beautiful, no woman would ever be a match for her? Or was he put off by her lack of formal education—after all, Marina was a law professor; he was a geologist. Whatever the reason was, she, the femme fatale, had failed to seduce the one man she really wanted to be with. The one she longed to touch. The one man whose kisses she dreamt about.

Now her ego needed some stroking. She knew where she'd get that, too. As soon as she got home, she'd call Lance Potter, arrange to meet him. Another candlelit dinner? A suggestion that he cook for her—he'd often bragged about his cooking expertise. Yes, that was the perfect idea.

There, in Lance's house, she would seduce the daylights out of him. Remembering that she'd lost interest in Lance, because she'd imagined a romance with Jonah, made her feel like kicking herself. *Fool.* Passing up one perfectly good man for another who wanted only friendship.

A passionate night with Lance would certainly push thoughts of Jonah and unrequited lust out of the picture. It was a good way of taking revenge on him for his indifference.

****

No man could resist her, Rose decided with satisfaction. Her black bodysuit and stretch leopard leggings were sure-fire seduction tools. As she drove out of Blake's Folly, she pictured the evening in front of her: soft music, candlelight, flowers on the table, a delicious dinner of exotic foods—Lance knew how much she liked things like that. The game of seduction: his eyes meeting hers, the inevitable current passing through them both.

She ran the images through her head, trying to warm her thoughts with them. For some crazy reason, they weren't having the desired effect. Sure, erotic anticipation was exciting—who was it who'd said "the best part of seduction is when you're going up the stairs"? How true. Often the anticipation was more exhilarating than the completion.

At the moment, however, the anticipation seemed to be missing. Why? Lance was sexy, gorgeous; she was certain he'd be a wonderful lover. So what was going on? Had her fascination for Jonah ruined her? Killed off her desire for any other man? How ridiculous.

Well, if the mental pizzazz wasn't there, she'd have to decide to get it back. She'd *convince* herself it was there. It was a matter of pride: she was tired of being crazy about an unavailable man. On the other hand, she didn't have to make a decision now, and she didn't *have* to make love with Lance. She'd see how things went, once she was in his presence. Sighing, she parked the car.

As soon as she walked into Lance's house and entered his spacious main room, she saw how far astray fantasy had led her. The dining room table wasn't set for a romantic meal: no tablecloth, no candles, and no flowers. No delicious odors floated in from the kitchen. The television was on, and Lance was happily ensconced on the sofa, watching the game, a bowl of popcorn on the table in front of him, a beer in one hand. Rose could hardly believe her eyes. This was a seduction scene? It was more like a normal evening in a dull marriage: hubby in front of the set, ignoring the "little woman."

Lance smiled up at her, patted the place next to him on the sofa, as if nothing were amiss, and this was the perfect way to receive a seductive lady. He had to be joking. Slowly, Rose shrugged off her fluffy coat, rounded the sofa, paused, waited for Lance to look at her, take in the sexy-as-hell outfit that left none of her soft curves to the imagination. Did he look up? Not at all. His eyes stayed riveted on the screen.

Incredible! Unenthusiastically, she sat down beside him. Waited some more. Would he snap off the set, turn to her, try to please her as usual? He didn't. Now, what was she supposed to do? Snuggle in beside him, dig into the popcorn, and watch the game? If that's what he expected, he'd chosen the wrong woman to do it with. He did know better. She was certain he did. What was going on?

"I'm starving," she said in a sultry little voice meant to get his attention. Perhaps he'd get up, concoct some wonderfully original cocktail, an aphrodisiac of some sort.

He still wasn't looking at her. "Have some popcorn. There's beer in the fridge."

"Beer and popcorn for dinner? Is this your latest gourmet experiment?"

Lance's eyes finally met hers, as calm as they usually were when meeting with friends in a public place. "I have some frozen pizzas we can heat up later." Then his attention went back to the set.

Rose sat there, stunned. Waited a few minutes. Then had to admit the obvious: Lance felt the same way she did: he wasn't the least bit interested in seduction. His apparent interest in her had been a game. She stood, went over to the chair where she'd left her coat, slipped it on. Lance still wasn't watching her, still wasn't paying her the slightest heed. He probably had no idea that she was now in the hallway, that she was heading out the front door, walking toward her car in the snowy street.

She stopped once, turned, half expecting him to rip open the door and come pounding down the path after her. The door didn't open. Her heart heavy, she climbed into the car, turned the key in the ignition, slowly began rolling down the road. Heading for Blake's Folly, end of the world that it was. "Nowhere land," she mumbled.

Then, quite suddenly, her dreary mood lifted. She

felt relieved. Relieved that she wasn't with Lance, wasn't seducing him. That her plan hadn't worked. She started laughing. At the situation. At herself. At Lance. At the wonderful thought that she was on her way home. If she had to spend tonight alone, she'd enjoy it perfectly. Pleased with her own company, as always.

****

Bright morning sunbeams danced across the well-worn wooden plank floor in Alice's house. Rose sat at the long wooden table in the vast yellow kitchen, while Noodle rolled on the floor with a black mutt named Killer and several other fat, happy rescue dogs. From the old iron stove, came the aroma of baking bread.

Alice's house was a haven in the desert, and her accomplishments were endless: she was a brilliant vegetarian cook; she had a degree in zoology; she had the wonderfully appealing writer Jace Constant pursuing her madly; and she was beautiful. Whereas she, Rose, was surrounded by men, and the two she particularly liked didn't take her seriously. Worse, they'd rejected her.

"Can you believe it? Jonah Livingstone isn't interested in me, and Lance Potter resisted my attempt at seduction. I've lost all my allure. I'm no longer desirable. I've finally become a wallflower, the woman no one wants. The invisible woman."

Alice, sitting across the table from her, roared with laughter, a sincere sound from deep in her belly.

Offended, Rose glowered. "What's so funny about failure?"

Alice shook her head. When her laughter receded, the big grin was still in place. "Have you started packing for your trip to Costa Rica with Tracey yet?"

Rose was silent for a long while. "That's not the same."

"How isn't it the same?"

"Because I never wanted to go to Costa Rica with Tracey," she said in a little voice. "Not really. I sort of played around with the idea that I might…"

"Aha."

"Aha, what?"

"So, you might fly off to some tropical paradise with Tracey. But first you went to Lance's house to seduce him. I guess Lance probably thinks you're going away with Tracey, right?"

"I suppose he might," Rose admitted begrudgingly.

"Jonah also thinks you're going to Costa Rica with Tracey?"

"Tracey announced it when we were all having lunch together at the Mizpah. And yes, it's true: I didn't get a chance to deny it. I sort of left it up in the air."

"Right. Every time you're with Jonah, Lance is also around. And Tracey. And Roy. And all the other men who adore you. And you're charming to all, flirtatious with all."

"Men like being flirted with; they like being toyed with. That's why they hang around me. Having 'pretend' rivals stimulates them. It reassures them too, because they can act like proud males and never have to commit to anything."

"Yes, you're probably right about that. On the other hand, how do you expect any one of them to take you seriously?"

"None of them *want* to take me seriously. They don't want me to take them seriously, either. It would make them feel threatened. This is the game of seduction, not permanence."

"You think so? Is that what you're really complaining about?"

Rose shrugged. No, she wasn't sure. She wasn't sure what Alice was getting at, either.

"Okay," Alice continued. "What if a man wanted something more intense with you? How would he go about it? From what you've told me, Jonah has made a lot of effort to be with you, discover who you are, and to show you the things that interest him, too."

"And?"

"Stop being obtuse, Rose. You've known Lance, and Tracey, and Roy for a long time. They've been seeing you with lots of men over the years—Rick Barker, Michael Dodd, Robbie James, to name a few. They are all men you flirt with. You don't take any of them seriously. Jonah doesn't know that. All Jonah sees is that you're surrounded by men, and he's part of the crowd. That's probably how Lance feels, too."

Rose ran her fingernail along a deep, ancient scratch on the tabletop. She knew Alice was right. "Okay. I give up. What am I supposed to do now?"

Alice smiled. "Do about what?"

Rose stared at her friend, her mind blank. What had she been talking about for the last half hour or more? What had she been explaining? Why didn't Alice understand that? "Oh," she said, finally. "I see what you mean. What is it I really want?"

"Exactly."

Lost in thought, Rose chewed her lip. Then sighed. "Do I want Lance, or Tracey, or Jonah, or the next man who comes trotting over the horizon, or a dream prince, or a kissable toad, or a white knight? Or more of the status quo."

Alice nodded. "Unless you don't know."

"Of course, I know. I want to be with Jonah. I want to spend time with him. I want to hear him play music. I want to wander over the freezing cold countryside with him and look for fossils, or sit in cafés with him, talking. I want to touch him so badly, my whole body aches…" She stopped. What was the point of dreaming, of hoping, or of revealing all of this to someone? How embarrassing. Alice could never understand what she was feeling, Rose was sure of it. "I know how childish I sound. Forgive me."

"Why does it sound childish? To me, it sounds like the beginning of love."

"To me too. That's what makes me so miserable. I've discovered that Jonah never cared for me in the way I hoped he would."

"How do you know? Look at the way you've handled things."

"I know. I've made a mess of everything. I keep a stable of men around me all the time. I didn't tell Tracey I definitely didn't want to go to Costa Rica with him. I drove to Lance's house with the intention of seducing him so I could stop feeling miserable about Jonah. And Jonah, what did I do with him? Nothing. Did I expect that, by some divine intuition, he'd know he was special to me?"

"You could remedy the situation, you know."

"Yes…well…I could *try* and remedy it. But there's no guarantee the remedy would work."

"Life never does have set guarantees."

Chapter Eighteen: Inside the Loft

"Jonah?"

"Rose."

"Uh, I'm, uh…in Reno at the moment. Actually, I'm in your neighborhood. In fact, I'm in front of your building. Are you busy?"

"No, I'm not busy."

"Can I come up to see you?"

"Come up to the loft? Yes…sure."

Had he hesitated? She was certain of it. Was he up there with another woman? She could picture that, too: wine on the table, soft lighting, the air of intimacy. Then she pushed the image out of her mind. So what if there was a woman with him? She could always say she was passing through town and wanted to say "hello."

"Do you want the code for the electronic keypad?"

"No, I don't need it. I remember it from when I came here with you last time." She felt like slugging herself. She sounded like a stalker, remembering the code, coming all the way here, to his loft, late at night.

"Fine." He didn't sound worried. "See you in a minute, then."

Rose tucked her telephone into her handbag, punched in 046J. Then, assailed by a million doubts, she tiptoed up the two flights of iron stairs leading to Jonah's floor. What if he really wasn't interested in her? Of course he was, she told herself. He wouldn't have made such an effort to be with her if he weren't. If she were wrong? Well, this was the moment of truth. After this evening, she'd know where she stood…more or less.

She raised her hand to knock at the heavy metal door and then stopped. What if he was annoyed that she had come here? She didn't have to take off her coat, did she? Show him the outfit she was wearing—an outfit that screamed seduction.

"Oh, stop being a coward," she muttered. Still, she waited, listening hard. Did she hear conversation on the other side of the door? No. So, he was probably alone. Probably…

She raised her hand, knocked.

The door opened, and he was standing in front of her, staring at her with surprised amusement, not annoyance. My, didn't he look wonderful. The sight of him was like a deep taste of rich red wine. His white shirt set off the ropy strength of his shoulders and the tawny hue of his skin; the tight jeans outlined the length of his legs. The natural scent of him was a heady musk.

He stepped aside. "Come in."

She entered, looked around the room. There was no other woman present, but the loft was transformed. No more boxes piled up, no heaped furniture. Books lined the finished wooden shelves along the far wall; a sofa and several armchairs stood on a Turkish carpet in the center of the room. The lighting was soft, seductive. Near the window, beside a music stand, was the cello.

"It looks great."

"Thanks." Although smiling and evidently pleased at her approval, he was watching her with undisguised curiosity. "This is quite an unexpected visit. What brings you to this part of the world on a Wednesday?"

Slowly, she turned back toward him. Met his eyes squarely. "I've come to seduce you," she answered, more than a little breathlessly.

"Ah." He stared at her for a minute, and then laughed softly. The sound shivered over her flesh, and the temperature in the room seemed to heat up by several degrees. Still, he made no move toward her.

What if he didn't want her? What if he considered this an intrusion? What if this whole idea was a bad mistake?

Then she stopped thinking and did what she was longing to do, anyway. With one step she closed the distance between them, reached up, undid the buttons on his shirt, ran her hands caressingly over the taut skin of his chest. The hiss of breath through his teeth was music to her ears. His eyes glittered, but he watched her, not moving.

Finally, after what seemed like an eternity, he reached out, pulled her into his arms, and brought his mouth down on hers with a passion that took her breath away. Her eyelids closed as if weighted, and she moaned softly.

"I know," he growled, his mouth against hers. "It feels so good."

The kiss turned into another, then another. Arching her hips, she pressed against him in a demand that was unmistakable, and feeling his pulsing hardness, liquid heat filled her belly. She needed him inside of her. But she could wait: she had to. This might be the only night she would ever have with Jonah, and she wanted it to be memorable. She wanted it to be an experience he would never be able to forget.

J. Arlene Culiner

Forcing herself to step back out of his embrace, she opened her coat, let it slide down over her arms. She watched his eyes take in the short, skin-tight black vinyl skirt, the black vinyl vest pushing her full breasts upward, and the heat in his eyes scorched her.

"I want you to undress." Her voice was so husky, she hardly recognized it. "I want to watch you. I want to see you naked."

He lifted his hand, let his fingers caress her rosy, kiss-softened lips, then move downward to the sweet hollow between her breasts.

She caught his hand, shook her head slowly. "No, this is my call. You first."

He hesitated, but briefly, then kicked off his shoes, slowly undid the remaining buttons on his shirt, let it drop on the floor. Undid the buckle of his belt, stepped out of his jeans, then his shorts, until he was standing naked before her in all his male glory. There was no doubt that he wanted her, and her own body throbbed with desire. She wanted—needed—to touch him, to taste him.

Her fingers trembled as she reached out, caressed his thighs, cupped his hard hot male flesh in both hands, then she bent down to take his fullness into her mouth. His fingers clutched in her hair, and his ragged groan of pleasure spurred her on as she slid down the length of him with her lips and tongue. Then, quite suddenly, he pulled her up beside him.

"Why…?"

"Didn't anyone ever tell you this sort of pleasure is interactive?" he insisted throatily. He reached for the front zipper of her vest, slowly slid it down, releasing her breasts. Then bending, he took each achingly sensitive nipple in his mouth, laved it, sent delicious frissons of pleasure throughout her body. Instinctively, her fingers gripped the hot, elastic skin of his back as his mouth moved lower, down her body, stopping at the waistline of the black skirt, working its way back up to her breasts again.

"This has to come off," he said. His fingers tugged at the skirt's zipper.

"It does," she sighed, her fingers helping his until she was standing in front of him, clad in her lacey garter belt and stockings.

"No underpants?" One eyebrow arched.

She laughed, but the sound ended in a gasp as his fingers went to the juncture of her thighs, parted them to seek out her moist center. She bucked against him, then raised one leg, coiling it around him to bring his sex to hers, aching for him to fill her.

"Not so fast," he said softly. "All this sexy stuff has to disappear, too."

"Don't you like the sexy stuff?" she murmured.

"I do, oh yes, I certainly do. But this is the first time, and I want to see, taste, make love to every inch of you. Cloth, even sexy cloth, is too much of a barrier." Deftly, the stockings and lace disappeared.

At first, he caressed her with his eyes, taking in the softness of her curves, the scoop of her waist, and the flare of her hips. "Beautiful," he murmured. Then, lifting her into his arms, he carried her across the broad space of the loft and into his bedroom. Laid her gently on his bed.

She reached for him, needing him, aching for him, but his mouth retraced the trail down over her breasts, to her belly, to the junction between her thighs, parting them to seek out her wetness, tightening the coils of passion searing through her.

"Jonah." His name was an ache of want on her lips. "Jonah, wait."

"For what?" His laugh was low, rich. "I've waited so long for this. To taste you. Be inside you."

The confession was music to her ears. Her own laughter, lascivious, deep, met his. "Then what *are* we waiting for?"

"Good question."

Pulling a small packet from the drawer in a table beside the bed, he sheathed himself and, lifting her hips, claimed her in one slow, smooth movement. She arched against him as he thrust deeper, setting a rhythm that she matched equally, driving them headlong to the satisfaction that came with explosive force. Left them clinging to each other as the waves of pure pleasure washed over them both.

They lay quietly until the world righted itself.

"Rose?" Jonah brushed sweat-soaked strands of hair from her cheek. "I'm sorry I went so fast. Did I hurt you?"

She kissed the crook of his neck, the soft skin under his ear. "You couldn't hurt me. I loved every minute of it."

"Then we'll have to do it all over again," he said, his voice teasing. "Take it slower. See which way we really prefer it."

She trailed a lazy finger over his taut nipple, followed it with her tongue. "Now, that sounds like an excellent proposition."

****

Bright morning sunlight danced across the love-tossed bedclothes. Rose slept softly, her beautiful shoulders cupped into his arm, her curls a tangle against the white pillow, her mouth sweet and love bruised. He could hardly believe that this night of lovemaking had really happened, that he hadn't fantasized holding her in his arms, tasting her, pleasuring her over and over. Finally. After all the long nights he had dreamt of doing that.

Except that the reality had been more powerful than what he'd imagined, and she was lovelier than he had anticipated. He loved the passion of her breasts, the slenderness of her waist, the full flare of her hips that curved to creamy thighs. She had given herself to him with no reticence, had demanded the same from him.

Now what? Where could this go? Where did he want it to go? What did he want to risk? His heart? His newly won freedom and independence?

She stirred beside him, opened eyes that filled with pure joy at finding him there, holding her close.

"Good morning," he said, kissing her gently.

"Morning already?"

"We did pass the night in a rather special way." Unable to resist—or was it to reassure himself that she really was there—he ran his hand down over her breasts and across her flat belly. Smiled when, instinctively, her hips arched toward him again.

"Voracious woman."

"Hmmm." She curled one leg over his hips so that her intimacy touched his, coaxing, promising.

He kissed her more deeply, curling her more closely into him, savoring the warmth of her skin, its natural scent. Then forced himself to pull back. "We should stop. For now, anyway."

Her eyes, blue, limpid, met his. Questioning.

"It's not that I don't want more," he said, already regretting that this night was over, that the real world was intruding on the magic. "But Sergei will be showing up in less than an hour."

"Sergei?"

"Sergei. Your musician friend."

She sat up abruptly, gawped at him, wide-eyed. "Sergei who plays the balalaika?"

"He's the only Sergei I know, so far."

"You're joking. Why is he coming here?"

"Because, on Saturday night, after you introduced us, we talked about music. He and Boris thought it would be interesting if we played together—balalaikas and my cello. I don't know the music, of course, but I'll try, play by ear. We'll see how it goes. If it works out, he invited me to come play with everyone at the Russian Club." He stopped, uncertain of her reaction, wondering if he had gone too far.

"You mean, on Saturday nights?"

"Unless you mind, that is."

"Why would I mind?"

"Because you might feel that I'm imposing myself on your life, crowding in on you."

"Why in heaven's name would I think that? There are masses of people who pack into the club every Saturday. Why do you think one more person would constitute a crowd?" Then her lips curved upward in a wholehearted smile. "Oh, Jonah, I think it's a wonderful idea."

"Good," he said, relieved.

Suddenly, her expression changed. "Wait a minute. You said Sergei is showing up here?"

He nodded. "In about forty minutes, now."

"Oh no." She leapt out of bed. "I have to get dressed, get out of here. Sergei, if he finds me here—I mean, he's so old-school, so old-fashioned. And…oh…oh no! If he sees the clothes I was wearing last night…he'll think I've been trolling the streets."

He stood, caught her in his arms again, ran his hands over her sleek back, over her rounded bottom, then briefly lifted her against him. "So, we'll have to take a rain check."

"Fine with me." Gently, she nipped the lobe of his ear with her little white teeth. "No, it sounds better than fine. It sounds like heaven."

Chapter Nineteen: Roses

He didn't call her later that day, and she tried not to feel disappointed. Why would he have? They had seen each other that morning. *And had spent last night together, making the most wonderful love.* Still, she couldn't help feeling discouraged when she climbed into her bed that night. How she would have liked him to be here, lying in her arms. Here, in her bed, with its silky pastel coverlet and satin sheets. Here, in her sexy secretive bedroom where the window's diaphanous curtains partially hid the dark desert sky, its moon sliver, its winking stars.

And in the morning when she woke, her arms reached for him, for he had been so present in her dreams, it was almost as if he had been there with her.

Ridiculous. Or was it? Why was she obsessed by Jonah Livingstone? The answer was so extremely simple, she was astounded she hadn't acknowledged the feeling before. Because she loved him. Deeply. She had probably begun falling in love with him the night he had first walked into her store. What she had classified as lust, a flirtation, a powerful attraction, a mere fantasy, a potential love story, had always been much more than she had allowed herself to admit. What could she do about it? Nothing. The next move was undeniably Jonah's.

She sat up, stretched her arms. Spied Noodle on the

floor beside the bed, lying on his doggie blanket. His golden eyes watched her with pure adoration, and his tail wagged with happiness.

"How easy metaphysical questions are for you canine critters," she told him. Noodle wagged his tail harder, in absolute agreement.

"Okay, you win. This is your big day."

She dressed warmly, pulled on her hiking boots, called Lucy Barnes who was, as usual, more than happy to run the shop for her. Then she and Noodle set out across the plain, taking the dusty forgotten trails once crisscrossed by the Paiute and Shoshone people, by settlers and pioneers, by miners, sheepherders, and cattle rustlers. The air was frosty, the ground hard. A faint wind rattled the dry stalks of low-lying shrubs, rubbing grasses in a percussive musical counterpoint. Sometimes, startled black-tailed jackrabbits abandoned shallow hollows at their approach, sped into the far distance on their long rangy legs. She saw cottontails too, recognized their zigzag run as they sought safety in the scrub.

"You have nothing to fear from me," she called to their retreating furry shapes. Noodle, although he made a vague, half-hearted attempt at chase, seemed to know that he was no match for such high-speed creatures.

With every determined step across the chilly plain, her thoughts were for Jonah, but they were beginning to take on a semblance of order. What did love mean to her? Did it mean she was finally ready to take the risk of everyday humdrum? Her heart told her she was. With Jonah, she was. Because life with him would never be humdrum. He was too alert, too passionate about so many things: his heritage, music, and prehistory, even this empty plain. He would always be stimulating.

She would always want him, his touch, his kisses, and their lovemaking. She would always need the fragrance of his skin, his presence. *You have it bad, poor woman*, she chided herself. The thought didn't worry her like it might once have.

What about Jonah? How did he feel? She still couldn't know that. Surely, their lovemaking had been as important to him as to her. Surely. She'd thought so the night before last when she'd lain in his arms, when he'd loved her body with his own. Was she so certain now? When would she hear from him? See him again? She didn't know that either, and there was nothing she could do about it. She'd played her wild card; the next move would, undeniably, have to be his.

It might not be soon. She had come to understand Jonah: he was a man who needed time. Ever since they'd met, he'd needed time: time in which to think about what they could share, about what they might mean to each other. Time in which to realize he was special to her? That she was important to him? That perhaps he could love her too?

How much time was that? What if she were wrong?

****

The Mizpah was a hive of industry. Tomorrow night was the big night, the Blake's Folly Get-Together, and the main room was being prepared for the affair. Rather faded, sometimes tattered streamers (the same ones were used each year), hung from every doorway, every archway, every window. Food was arriving too, supplementing the Mizpah's offerings on this special occasion, and all the local females (also a few males) were determined to show off their prowess at cooking and baking. True, some of the bakery efforts were slightly lopsided; others looked doubtful at best; but there was a small mountain of the stuff accumulating. Tomorrow, more would arrive—dishes that needed to be prepared at the last minute. For the moment, though, there was enough food to send half the state toddling merrily home, burping heartily, with full bellies and high cholesterol counts.

Rose, absolutely hopeless in matters of cuisine either fine or basic, reluctantly tried to make herself useful, placing cookies on trays, arranging cutlery, stacking plates, but her incompetence couldn't match the efficiency of those more domestic. Soon, she was shooed off—much to her own relief—so she joined Sly Grimes who was up at the bar, drinking a beer.

"Ready for the big concert tomorrow, Sly?"

"Yeyay-ass," said Sly, in his usual hermetic personal lingo. "Got somma good ni-yew sty-uff."

"Mmm." Rose decided that onomatopoeia was the most judicious tool for this level of communication. She wasn't at all sure she'd understood the slightest word Sly had uttered. She wished he would speak to her in a normal language. They might have a sensible conversation if he did. She decided to make an effort.

"Sly? I've often wondered how you now feel about the old days. About the time when you were in San Francisco and trying to break into the music scene. Do you ever regret leaving the city, coming back to Blake's Folly?"

Sly squinted at her, obviously too surprised to answer. Either no one had ever asked him that question before, or the memory of days gone by was too rusty to get into dialogue gear again.

"I mean," she continued. "I don't regret coming back at all. I'm not sorry that I lived that pop star life, but I wouldn't want to do it over again. I certainly don't want to sing that sort of music, anymore. Which is why I always avoid the subject whenever you bring it up."

"You totally gave up singing," said Sly in a perfectly normal sentence, with a perfectly normal local accent, and with most of the grammatical elements in their proper place. She must have shocked him to his core.

"No, I didn't give it up." She took a big breath and decided to confide, even if the information spread over the whole community faster than dust in a prairie tornado. "I still sing. Almost every Saturday night. In Reno. I sing Russian folk music."

"Y'all don't say."

She smiled. "I do say. I don't spread the word around, because I don't want my mother showing up. You'll keep it a secret, right?"

"Cross mah heart. Akshully, that's why I kep' on askin' you if you din wanna sing with the Old Boys. I didn't like the idea that you didn't sing anymore. You did it real good back then. It seemed a waste for you to stop. Now, I won't keep a-gittin' on yer case about it anymore."

She reached over, impulsively squeezed his arm. "That's so sweet of you, Sly. Thanks for your concern."

He looked mighty chuffed. Then shifted from one foot to the other. "No, to answer your question, I don't miss the old days either. Goin' to the city, trying to make it big, was jus' somethin' I had to do. It was no good, as you know. I ended up loadin' cans in a supermarket. So I gave up, came back. And you know what? It's as good singing and playing here in town or in the other bars in the area, though we don't make much cash to speak of. Maybe it's better doing it this way. Doing it our own way. Doing it small. Learning to believe in what we do again."

"Oh yes, I understand that perfectly."

"Funny, ain't it? Sometimes we don't know what we got until we open our eyes, take a good look at how lucky we really are."

"Amen," she said and realized how sincerely she meant it.

****

A faint pink wash stained Lucy Barnes's cheeks when Rose and Noodle returned to the shop. The woman looked guilty as hell. What had she been up to? Rose trusted Lucy. She knew she would never pilfer the cash register (when there was anything in there to pilfer). She would never steal clothes, or shoes, or old hats, either. Where would she wear them? Everyone in Blake's Folly would be certain to comment on the poor woman's new apparel if she did.

Rose pretended not to notice anything untoward in Lucy's demeanor, although she did quickly glance around the shop to see if anything was amiss. Her eyes caught the long white box lying on the little round table near the plush armchair. A florist's box. Rose's heart leapt. Flowers? From whom?

"That came for you about an hour ago," said Lucy, and blushed again. "Problem was, Ma Handy was in the shop at the same time. She claimed she was looking for a red scarf to wear tomorrow night, so I started digging around in that trunk near the window—yes, I know it was silly of me to let her pull the wool over my eyes: Ma never buys anything in this shop. And while my back was turned, she fussed around with that carton."

"She would, the nosy old cow." Then Rose noticed that the little strip of tape holding the box closed was slightly askew. So the awful Ma Handy had taken a peek and collected information for the gossip machine. Rose couldn't be bothered feeling annoyed.

Holding her breath, she lifted the half-stuck tape, opened the box, and folded back the layers of tissue paper. Inside, were the exquisite blooms of a dozen long-stemmed red roses. Her fingers trembled slightly as she opened the little white envelope nestled between the leaves, took out the card. On it, was simply one word: Jonah.

Picking up one bloom, she inhaled its deliciously creamy scent. Red roses? Her heart turned over. Everyone and his uncle knew what red roses meant, didn't they?

She then noticed that the box contained something else. A tiny packet wrapped in red tissue paper. She tore away the paper and found a tiny, rounded Russian doll, a *matryoshka*, exquisitely and elaborately painted. She cradled the little figurine in the palm of her hand. Where in heaven's name had Jonah found her? Her heart swelled as hope flooded through her veins. No, she hadn't been mistaken.

Chapter Twenty: The Get-Together

Jonah leaned against the wall of the Russian Club and surveyed the crowd, not understanding one word, of course. Who would have thought he had to learn Russian to function in one tiny corner of Reno, Nevada? His heart was thumping. He felt as nervous as a music student about to play in his first recital, not like a man who had been playing for the public with his chamber group for years now. Would he make a fool of himself up on the stage? Would everyone know he was an impostor, that he was faking his way through the melodies that were so new to him? Still, he felt proud that Sergei and the other musicians had let him join them—after two days of rather grueling rehearsals.

At the same time, despite his nervousness, the latent excitement in the hall touched him too. No doubt on every Saturday evening, there was this same charge of electricity, this same anticipation. No doubt. That was why Rose was drawn to the place, why she had wanted to sing again after coming back to Nevada.

Where the hell was she? Why was it taking her so long to get here? He had to see her; he wanted to see her. He wanted her to be proud of him. He wanted to leave this hall tonight with her in his arms, to make love with her as he had the other night—at least that much was clear to him. Where was their relationship going? Was it a relationship, or a short-term passion? He didn't know how Rose felt, but he knew how he did. These three days without her had given him all the room for thought that he'd needed, and he was ready to fight for what he wanted. For what he hoped she wanted, too.

Frustrated, he pushed away from the wall, picked up his cello, headed for the dais. Several of the musicians had already arrived, and they were either tuning their instruments up, or taking them out of their cases. Hearing the tinkling balalaikas dispelled the rest of his nervousness, turned it into excitement.

Tonight was his debut performance. Tonight was a night he wouldn't want to miss for anything in the world. It was unusual to include classical western instruments into balalaika orchestras, but it was done from time to time in Russia. Sergei said he considered it a worthy experiment here in the club.

The room was filling up fast, and the noise was deafening. Most of the chairs were occupied. Again, his eyes searched the crowd for Rose. Surely, it was unusual for her to be so late. Should he call her, see if everything was all right? If he did, though, his presence wouldn't be a surprise, and he'd wanted to surprise her. He wanted to keep on surprising her, too, the way she constantly surprised him.

Perhaps something had gone wrong. A flat tire? A breakdown? Unable to wait for a moment longer, he approached Sergei.

"What time does Rose usually arrive?"

"Rose? She always comes early." Sergei shrugged. "But she won't be here tonight."

"What?" Jonah peered at the man, lost for words.

"No, she isn't coming in this week. There's something going on out in that place she lives in."

"In Blake's Folly?" What the hell could be going on there? Then he remembered: the Blake's Folly Get-Together. He'd forgotten all about it.

"Yes, that's what she said. Some event she can't miss. She'll be here next week. Don't worry." Sergei smiled. "So…how do you feel? Ready for your big debut tonight? We'll be starting in around twenty minutes or so. Don't worry. It'll go well. You'll fit in fine."

****

In her high heels, her sedate, yet clinging, black dress, Rose knew exactly how sexy she looked. It was all a question of underplay, of knowing how to move, of a come-hither look, all of which she had down to perfection. That was on the outside. Deep inside, she was tied in knots.

Her usual gentlemen callers were here at the Get-Together—Tracey, Roy, and Lance—and they weren't the only men in the room who were watching with wistful or lustful eyes. One person was missing—Jonah—the one person she longed to see. She wanted to be with him. She wanted to feel his warmth under her fingertips, feel his mouth on hers. But he wasn't here, and there was nothing she could do about that.

She was being silly, and she knew it. Why would Jonah bother coming to the Blake's Folly Get-Together? This was a local affair, and despite all the excitement, muss, and fuss, when you let the scales fall from your eyes, you could see it was pure backwoods kitsch. The music was appalling—Sly Grimes and the Old Boy's Band had, so far, destroyed the "Tennessee Waltz," bungled "Oh Suzanna" in a hopelessly sadistic way, were now going for a full kamikaze hit at "I

Remember You." Worse than the horrendous noise level, was the local idea of party togs: better-dressed ancestors were probably spinning at high velocity in their graves at this exact moment.

Lance appeared in front of her, held out his hand. "Shall we dance?"

She wrinkled her nose. "If you think it's possible." Curling her fingers through his, she allowed him to lead her to the back of the room where the racket was less intolerable and there was a reasonable chance of moving. Lance took Rose skillfully in his arms, and he even found a recognizable beat they could dance to. Then again, Lance was such a wonderful dancer, he could waltz a three-footed woman to a cacophony of alley cats in a rain barrel. She let herself relax in his protective, comforting embrace.

"You're looking ravishingly beautiful tonight," he said softly, his mouth against her hair.

Rose pulled back slightly and met his eyes squarely. "Do I? I thought I didn't interest you."

His eyes were amused. "What gave you that idea? Because I didn't leap on you when you came to my house in that sexy, almost irresistible getup?"

"Yes," she answered evenly. "Exactly for that reason. Irresistible, you say? You resisted very well indeed."

His eyes flashed. "Don't underestimate your power as a femme fatale, sweetheart. Resisting you was hard. Still, I knew that taking you to bed was definitely not the right thing to do. The way I behaved wasn't right either. I know that, too, and I want to apologize."

"Oh." She couldn't manage anything better.

"Oh, what?"

"Simply oh."

"Look, Rose? I was intrigued when you called me and invited yourself to my house that night. The more I thought about it, the more uncomfortable I felt. Because that's not your style."

"What isn't my style?"

"Being so direct. You like toying with men, flirting with them, being admired, being invited out for romantic dinners. You also like men to do all the proposing. I'll admit I was flattered that, in this particular case, you were the one to instigate things. You are very seductive, very sexy, and very desirable. However, it struck me—before you arrived—that there was nothing personal in your visit."

"What's that supposed to mean?" She tried to sound shocked, but wasn't convinced she succeeded. He was right, of course. One hundred percent correct. She had gone to see Lance on the rebound, and he'd realized it. What bad behavior. She felt ashamed of herself.

"If I'd thought you were there for me, I wouldn't have hesitated. I would have enjoyed making love with you. You see, we're both one of a kind in that way. I love women; I love talking to women; I love holding them in my arms, dancing with them. I love making love with them. You're the same sort of person. You love men; you love being with us; and I don't doubt for a minute that you thoroughly enjoy making love with us. That's wonderful. And gratifying."

The music came to an abrupt, horribly dissonant halt. Rose dropped her arms, stared up at Lance. "But?"

He laughed shortly. Then keeping her hand in his, he led her off the dance floor. "Don't look so defensive.

J. Arlene Culiner

There's nothing wrong with being the sort of people we are. Sometimes, though—and rarely—something wonderful happens between two people. Something quite unique, quite special. For quite a while now, I've sensed there's that something special between you and Jonah, even if neither one of you has actually come out and admitted it. Then, when I saw you together at the Russian Club, when I saw how you looked at him, how he watched you, how much he wants to be part of your world, I realized that there is—or could be—that intense, magical feeling between the two of you."

Rose stared at him. Jonah wanted to be part of her world? Maybe. Maybe not. Or in a way. He *did* want to be part of the Russian Club; he *had* promised a rain check on lovemaking. Was that being part of someone's life? Or was it a romantic interlude? She opened her mouth to protest, but Lance gently pressed one finger to her lips.

"Let me finish, Rose. Look, I don't know why the two of you aren't together right now. The other night, I realized your visit had nothing to do with me, and everything to do with the fact that you weren't with Jonah. So, I chose not to take you up on your offer. When I'm with a woman, I like to have her full attention. That doesn't mean that something can't happen between the two of us one day in the future. Who knows? It means that now isn't the right time."

Wordlessly, she nodded. How right he was. How understanding. How forgiving. She'd wanted to use him, and he wasn't in the least bit resentful. Would she have been so forgiving if a man had done the same thing to her? Tried to use her as a substitute? She doubted it.

"Would you like something to drink?" There was no reproach in his voice, no resentment.

"Yes, please. A glass of wine would be lovely."

"Chardonnay, as usual?"

"As usual."

He turned, prepared to head for the bar, but she caught his arm before he could take two steps. "Lance?"

His eyes smiled. "Rose?"

"Thank you." She took a deep breath. "And I do care for you in some quite wonderful way; you know that, don't you? Knowing you, seeing you, talking with you is important to me."

"I know, Rose. I feel the same way about you. Let's wait, see where life brings us."

"Wherever it does, let's not lose what we have, okay?"

"It's a deal." He gazed at her for a moment, his eyes warm. Then bent, kissed her, a gentle, brief brush, before heading in the direction of the bar.

****

Jonah shouldered his way through the crowd. He hadn't known there would be so many people here tonight. He should have expected it, of course. The Get-Together had been the major topic of conversation in Blake's Folly for weeks now. Besides, where else could anyone go when you needed a little contact out here? How could he have forgotten the event? *Idiot.*

He didn't have to look for Rose; he saw her immediately. Before he saw her, he felt her presence, as if some part of him functioned on a unique intimate sonar that honed out everyone else.

She was on the other side of the immense room,

and Lance Potter was standing beside her. Of course, he would be. If Lance weren't there, Tracey would be, or every Bob, Dick, and Harry, in the state of Nevada. As usual. There was always an army of men to fight through. But this time, he wouldn't be put off by anyone. Not until he and Rose got things straight.

He doubted that she showed up at every man's abode the way she'd shown up at his three nights ago. If she did, he seriously doubted she made love with them the way she had with him. It wasn't likely. The kind of intimacy and trust they'd shared wasn't possible without a hell of a lot of feeling behind it.

Rose and Lance seemed to be engaged in an intense sort of conversation. Then, as he circumnavigated an odd-looking Blake's Folly resident precariously balancing a drinks tray and dressed in a violent concoction of mauve and pink net, he saw Lance bend down and kiss Rose.

The bastard. What was worse, Rose didn't look at all unhappy about it. So maybe he had been wrong? Maybe she *was* the sort of woman who could make love with many men with that same warm passion she'd showed him.

Then he pushed the negative thoughts out of his mind. You had to know when to have faith in people, when to trust your own instincts. You had to take risks too—the risk of being wrong, the risk of being rejected, the big risk of letting yourself fall in love—if you hoped to win.

Ten more steps and a considerable amount of elbowing through the crowd…finally, here she was, right in front of him. Staring up with what he could only interpret as wonderment. And pleasure. Something else too…

"Jonah," she breathed. "What are you doing here at the…I mean, I didn't…"

He looked at her, drinking in the sight of her, taking pleasure in her nearness, her scent. Her skin. Her aura. "You aren't going to Costa Rica," he said, his voice gruff. It wasn't a question. More of an order.

She didn't look shocked. Her eyes were that pellucid soft blue he loved. And so warm. So hopeful. Slowly, she shook her head. "No. I'm not," she said simply.

"Good." His heart was pounding. Filled with hope. *Slowly, take it slowly*, he ordered himself. *Don't ruin this*. He'd accepted, beyond any doubt, that she was as essential to him as fresh air and cool water, and he would fight for her, if need be. "Shall we dance?" he asked quietly.

"Yes, please."

"Please?" He pulled her into his arms, folding her against him, although the music was appalling—a strange half dirge, half fugue, in no identifiable key. He could feel the pounding of her heart against his, the warmth of her breath against his neck. Then, she moved in closer still, just as he hoped she would, pressing into him until they were hardly moving, but melding together until it was no longer a dance, but a wonderful continuation of their lovemaking.

"Rose?"

"Here I am."

He pulled back slightly, looked down at her. "I want you in my life. I want to be in yours."

Her lips curved upward, and her eyes blazed. "I want that too," she said softly. "Very much."

"Good. That's settled."

"Finally."

"We do love each other, don't we?" He hoped he wasn't fooling himself, that he hadn't let hope destroy any sense of reality. The depth of feeling he saw etched into her every feature, made his heart turn over.

"Yes, I'm certain we do."

He felt like roaring with joyful laughter, but he still had to keep his head for a few moments longer. "There are complications, of course. How do you feel about life in a loft in Reno?"

"How do you feel about life in a disused furniture workshop in Blake's Folly? Or being part owner of a dog called Noodle?"

He smiled, lifted his hand, let his fingers trace the fragile line of her jaw. "You think there's an easy way we can do all of those things?"

"I'm pretty sure there is."

"It'll work between us, won't it?"

"It will." She teased him with her eyes. "If we're good, that is."

"Oh, that we are," he growled. "We're very, very good."

A word about the author...

Writer, photographer, social critical artist, musician, and occasional actress, J. Arlene Culiner was born in New York and raised in Toronto. She has crossed much of Europe on foot, has lived in a Hungarian mud house, a Bavarian castle, a Turkish cave-dwelling, on a Dutch canal, and in a haunted house on the English moors. She now resides in a 400-year-old former inn in a French village of no interest and, much to local dismay, protects all creatures, especially spiders and snakes. She enjoys incorporating into short stories, mysteries, non-fiction, and romances, her experiences in out-of-the-way communities, and her conversations with strange characters. http://www.j-arleneculiner.com

Jap Hardy's story in Chapter Fourteen was inspired by an interview recorded by Nell Murbager in *Desert Magazine*, October 1955.

Murbager, Nell. "They Found New Wealth in Fairview." *Desert Magazine*, October 1955.
https://forgottennevada.org/sites/files/195510-DesertMagazine-1955-October%20Stratton%20Article.pdf

www.ingramcontent.com/pod-product-compliance
Lightning Source LLC
Chambersburg PA
CBHW070459260626
47161CB00004B/1372